Return to Tulsa
The Tulsa Series #4
Norma Jean Lutz

Return to Tulsa

ISBN: 978-1-947397-52-1

Return to Tulsa originally published by Barbour Publishing, Inc., 1997.

Table of Contents

Note from The Author
Regarding the Tulsa Series

The 4-title Tulsa series has had a long and interesting journey. In the late 1990s, I had just completed the last of four contemporary romance novels for Barbour Publishing's *Heartsong* line. At that time, I was approached by my editor at Barbour to submit ideas to him for historical fiction.

Because I've lived in the Tulsa area for most of my adult life, I knew a little bit about the infamous Tulsa Race Riot of 1921. But honestly, at that time, no one talked much about it. (That later changed as survivors began to speak up.) I knew that that event would serve as the backdrop for my historical, Christian, Tulsa series.

The very same day that my editor asked me for historical fiction ideas, I sat down and wrote out thumbnail sketches for all four titles. He liked the ideas and offered a 4-book contract.

All four, then, were originally published through Barbour's *Heartsong* line where they enjoyed immense popularity. (I still have file folders full of fan letters.)

Later, when the idea of eBooks was in its infancy, an independent group offered to publish my series digitally. As often happens in the publishing industry, the whole thing fell apart due to 1) being ahead of the curve regarding digitally-produced books, and 2) poor business management.

And, yes, yet another group purporting to be an independent publisher, also had their hands in the pie. That too fell apart.

Discouraging to say the least.

The Tulsa Series languished until I recently resurrected them and placed them on Amazon's Kindle. Even with that, little was done to promote the titles.

But this is a new day!

Presently, the four titles are decked out in delightful new covers, plus all will now be available in both print *and* digitally.

I trust as a reader, you will enjoy these stories as much as I enjoyed researching and writing them.

You can connect with me here:

normajean@beanovelist.com

http://www.beanovelist.com/

https://www.facebook.com/BeANovelist/

http://www.cleanteenreads.net/

https://www.facebook.com/CleanTeenReadsNet/

NUWS Link, Inc. Publishing

8703-R. North Owasso Expressway

Ste. 143

Owasso, OK 74055

Chapter 1

A hush fell over the audience crowded into the Oklah Theater as the electric lights slowly dimmed. Clarette hurried up the stairs in the near-darkness to the first balcony. Whispering apologies, she stepped on a few toes and pushed through to her front row seat. Scowling glances shot her way as she fished in her bag for her note pad and pencil. Paper rustled as she flipped to a clean page.

She nodded and smiled at Mr. and Mrs. Jess Overlees in their special box seat, and Mr. and Mrs. Frank Phillips in their box, then turned to glance over at Mr. and Mrs. H.V. Foster in their box. All of the *moneyed* people of the area had made their appearance for the evening.

The half-rate vaudeville act that was to open the show wasn't worth watching. No one Clarette knew in New York would have crossed the street to watch it. But here in Bartlesville, Oklahoma, the folks were glad to get most anything in the way of entertainment. Case in point was Ruby Darby whom they called the "Queen of the Oil Fields." Though Darby's musical comedy troupe impressed the locals, Clarette didn't even want to review it for the *Courier*, a weekly newspaper, which she and husband, Erik, published.

Erik, ever on the lookout for the least bit of news to garner more subscribers chided her about it. "You don't have to like Miss Darby," he told her in his usual patient manner, "our readers love her."

"She sings as though she were tone-deaf," Clarette protested.

But in the end Erik won out because deep down Clarette truly wanted to see their struggling paper make it. Even if it meant writing good reviews for less-than-mediocre stage stars.

She had to admit tonight would be quite different. Tonight's main attraction was Oklahoma's own favorite son, Will Rogers, which meant standing-room-only in the small theater. Excitement had been building all week as the oil-town population had done themselves proud rolling out the red carpet for the famed humorist.

Remembering the times she'd caught Will's appearances at the Ziegfeld Follies in New York, she knew they were in for a delightful evening. How she wished Erik could have come, but he was busy working at the *Courier* office. And even if he weren't all tied up with ad layouts and copy work, they couldn't have afforded the price of a ticket. Clarette was on the front row of the first balcony only because of her press pass.

The vaudeville troupe turned out to be just as Clarette had expected. She scribbled notes in her pad in the semi-darkness, barely bothering to look down at what she wrote.

The sight of Will sauntering onto the stage, calmly twirling his lariat, sent the thousand-plus Bartians into a frenzy. They jumped to their feet and nearly brought down the house with thunderous applause and hoots and cheers. Will stopped the twirling, pulled off his hat, scratched his head, and gave his lop-sided grin.

When it was quiet, he quipped, "Think I'll sit down now. I got no guarantee I'll get that response after I'm finished." But the applause broke out again. Local boy makes good. Although Will wasn't from Bartlesville, his family's farm was in the area near Oologah, and Clarette knew the entire state claimed Will as their very own.

She watched mesmerized as he moved from simple rope tricks to the more difficult. Spinning the rope vertically he jumped in and out of the wide loop as he moved across the stage with skill and grace. Two ropes, one spinning in each hand, were passed behind his back, then switched to opposite hands and he never missed a beat.

Will's famous quips and one-liners kept the audience roaring with laughter throughout the performance. He enjoyed poking fun at those who'd gained sudden wealth in the fertile oil fields. Plump Vernon Foster laughed louder than anyone. Clarette studied the two Foster daughters, Ruth and Marie, wondering if they chafed against the phony veneer of wealth as Clarette had when she was younger.

The grand finale of the show consisted of Will spinning a ninety-foot rope out over the heads of those in the audience. They loved it.

Guessing that there might be two or three curtain calls, Clarette closed her notebook and slipped out when the curtain rang down the first time. Again, raising the ire of those who were stomping and clapping and cheering, she edged her way to the aisle, went out the front door of the Oklah, and down the side alley toward the stage door. She promised Erik she'd try to get an interview backstage. They'd received word that Will was catching a train directly after the show, so time was limited.

She was sure someone from the *Magnet*, Bartlesville's daily, would have the same idea, and she was right. Young Joe Barber was standing at the stage door knocking as she approached.

Joe had always been congenial to Clarette, which she appreciated. They met often at events around the Osage country and she appreciated the fact that he never acted as though he were a competitor. She'd told Erik once that when they could afford a reporter she'd like to hire Joe away from the *Magnet*.

"Evening, Mrs. Torsten," Joe said touching his hat.

"Hi, Joe. What'd you think of the show?"

Joe grinned and shook his head. "Can't nobody make fun of President Harding and congress, and get away with it, the way Will does."

Just then the door opened and the wrinkled face of Borger Linahan peeked out. "Just you two?" he asked. In Bartlesville, Clarette never needed to show her press card, she was known all over town.

"Just us two for now," Joe replied. "But the whole town'll be swarming out here when that final curtain goes down."

"Hurry then," he said, waving them in. He looked out again and then quickly closed the door and slipped the bar down in place. "Can't be too careful," he said giving them a toothless grin.

Covering the news in this small burg was so different than the dog-eat-dog ways of New York, and yet at times Clarette still missed the excitement of her home city.

Backstage was crowded with workers and members of the vaudeville troupe. As the applause continued to reverberate throughout the theater, some of the troupe members, still clad in gaily-colored costumes, peered through the curtains marveling at the reception Will was receiving.

"Ain't he sumthin'?" Borger muttered shaking his head. "Ain't he just sumthin'?" They followed him down a set of stairs to the dressing rooms. "And young Will ain't never forgot where he come from neither. Still just as common as a wore-out boot. Eh, watch your step there."

He paused at the foot of the stairs to direct them to Will's dressing room.

"Will he be easy to interview?" Joe wanted to know. Clarette noted a nervous edge to his voice.

"Pshaw," Borger fairly spat the word. "Ain't nothing a'tall to talk to Will. Not like that puffed peacock Tom Mix. I knowed Tom when we was together out at the old 101-ranch bulldogging calves. Now all this moving-picture nonsense has plum went to his head."

The old man stopped at the door on which a massive garland of flowers hung. Pointing to the flowers he gave another toothless grin and said, "We done it up nice, didn't we?"

"You did just fine, Borger," Clarette assured him. "I'm sure Mr. Rogers is quite impressed.

Pushing the door open, he motioned the two reporters to go inside. "You can wait in here. I figure Will'll be along directly."

"I figure he will," Clarette said, not meaning to mock. She sat down on the overstuffed settee but Joe opted to pace.

"Calm down, Joe."

"I can't Mrs. Torsten. I've never been so nervous."

"He's just a man."

"Easy for you to say. You've probably talked to lots of stars when you were on the paper in New York. This is all new to me."

"You heard what Borger said—comfortable as a wore-out boot." She chuckled at the apt description. "Why a few years ago, he was practically your neighbor."

"Not mine. I come here from Missouri."

"Still..." Clarette started, but the noise at the door interrupted them. She was concerned that the cub reporter was going to faint dead away. His face took on a definite pallor as the door opened and in walked Will, his hat in his hand and the lariat slung over his shoulder.

"Howdy there," he said giving them a wide grin. As he removed his hat, a shock of hair fell carelessly across his forehead.

Borger was directly behind Will. "I done told them you're in a mighty big rush to get to the train station, Will."

Will nodded and smiled again. "Thanks Borger. You've been a great help."

Clarette was pulling her note pad out of her bag, as Joe nervously fished in his pocket for a crumpled piece of copy paper.

Following introductions, Will pulled a stool over from against the wall and sat down. "Now what can I do for you fine folks?"

Clarette conducted most of the interview as Joe was still beside himself with wonder. She asked all the general questions—

"How does it feel to be home?"

"What are your immediate plans?"

"Where are you going from here?"

"What does the year of 1922 hold for you?"

While Clarette wasn't sure how comfortable an old boot might be, she quickly felt at ease with Will Rogers. They learned he was on his way to Hollywood and hence the short stay in Oklahoma.

"They just keep asking me to make more moving pictures, and I don't aim to give 'em time to change their minds," he quipped.

When Clarette asked a few questions about the *Follies*, Will looked directly at her. "You sure don't sound like you're from around here. You from back East?"

She nodded. "New York."

"What part?"

Clarette hesitated a moment. Very few people in Bartlesville knew she was the daughter of Johannes Vanderpool of the Vanderpool Silk Company. Nor that she grew up in Hamptonwood, New Jersey surrounded by opulence. "I lived in Brooklyn for a time," she replied, then quickly added, "And worked as a reporter for the New York *American*."

"Good for you," he said with a chuckle. "That's a pretty fair-minded paper—considering."

Clarette thought back to last summer when she attempted to cover the Tulsa race riot. She had all the first-hand stories and photos, but the *American* refused to carry the scoop she'd uncovered. "Considering," she repeated. Considering that most all newspaper these days were corporately owned and few individual thinkers were involved. Her father had stated that fact to her many times.

Deftly, Clarette guided Will back to answering questions about himself—tidbits that she knew their readers would want to know. Joe mostly listened and took notes. Although Clarette realized she was aiding and abetting the competition, she really didn't mind. In a way it gave her a good feeling to help this young man.

Presently, Joe pulled out his pocket watch to glance at it. "Yikes," he said. Then grew crimson to tops of his ears. "Excuse me Mr. Rogers, but my boss at the *Magnet* said I was supposed to get this back to the office by ten-thirty and it's most nearly eleven."

"Well then, you just scoot along," Will said with a chuckle. "We sure don't want you getting in trouble."

Joe nervously shook hands with Will and made his exit.

Clarette had hoped against hope she'd have a few minutes alone with the star, and now the Lord had perfectly orchestrated the moment.

Presently Will's wife, Betty, came in and was introduced to Clarette. Her rose-beige crepe de chine frock with matching hat and gloves created an unpretentious statement of style. The charming fox collar clasped at the neck completed the ensemble perfectly. Like her husband, Betty Rogers was home folk and was as unpretentious as Will's scrubby leather chaps, which he began unstrapping.

Handing the heavy chaps to his wife, he said, "Mrs. Torsten here used to work on the *American*."

His wife raised her brows. "A New Yorker? My, how fortunate you are to have such a fine career. Women are doing so many more things nowadays than when I was younger."

"Mr. Rogers," Clarette said closing her notebook.

"Will," he corrected. "Mr. Rogers is my father."

She smiled. "Will, I know you've been around New York for years and you know a lot of people." She paused, thinking she must now sound as nervous as Joe. Taking a little breath, she plowed forward.

"I'm working on a play script that I feel sure would be great for Broadway. I've attended the theater since I was a small child and..." She paused, realizing that wasn't the right tack. Will was looking at her intently with eyes twinkling. How many people came at him for favors each time he performed? "Would you read the first act and suggest a name of someone in New York I might send it to?"

"Will?" Betty pointed to the gold wrist watch on her arm. "The train. It's getting late."

Will sat back down on the stool. "Mrs. Torsten..."

"Clarette."

"Clarette, let me suggest something. I don't want to take your script, for the simple reason I might lose it or forget clean all about it. But why don't you finish your play and produce it right here in the Oklah? Start your own little theater company in this town. These people need what you have to offer. Besides that, there's a great deal of raw material at your fingertips, not to mention a few wealthy people who might be interested and jump on such a project like a chicken on a June bug."

She let his words soak in. It was an interesting thought that had never occurred to her before. "I don't think Jesse Overlees is very interested in serious drama," she said. Jesse owned the Oklah Theater and Clarette happened to know he ran it his own way.

"Well, then," Will drawled, "the town can build their own theater."

The idea went off inside her like nitroglycerine shooting an oil well. She jumped to her feet. "That's a marvelous plan. I might just do that." She shook Will's hand and then Betty's. "Good luck with your next moving picture," she told him.

"Thank you kindly. Hollywood's not all that different from Broadway," he told her, "but at least it's warmer in California."

She thanked him again, and made her way through the now-quiet backstage area. In the alley way, she pushed through the gathering crowd. Hundreds of fans waited to catch a glimpse of their hero before he hurried away to the train station.

Street lights glowed softly overhead as Clarette walked down Johnstone Street past the Avaneda Hotel, past Zofness Brothers Clothiers south to Fifth. While Bartlesville was every bit as thriving as Tulsa, the Bartians didn't seem to be as anxious to build tall building as the Tulsans. After being in Bartlesville for nearly a year, Clarette had decided early on that she much preferred Tulsa. But she'd never tell Erik so.

If only they hadn't riled up the Klan in that area. She mentioned to Erik once that the Klan was everywhere in Oklahoma, revealing the barest hint that she'd like to go back to Tulsa. He didn't pick up on it; or *acted* as though he didn't pick up on it. Instead he continually told her how he loved having his own paper to run. And she knew he loved being back where he'd grown up.

She often heard the story of how Erik's father had come to the small town situated on the horseshoe bend of the Caney River, before the streets were paved, before the automobile arrived, and before the oil had been discovered. In the months since she'd become Mrs. Erik Torsten, she'd learned much about this wild country of Osage and Washington Counties.

Turning off Johnstone onto Fifth, she slowed her steps and studied the small storefront with the sign, Bartlesville *Courier* out front. She considered whether or not to tell Erik her latest plan. She often drove her husband into a tailspin with her wild ideas. At times she wondered if he wished he'd married a small-town girl who could cook and clean and sew buttons on his shirt. Although Clarette was making some effort at doing all those things, her heart was never in it. There were so many other things in life to do.

Now she had yet another delightful project to pursue.

Chapter 2

The lights in the newspaper office were aglow, casting yellow beams onto the sidewalk outside. Peering in the window, Clarette could see Erik sitting at the desk bowed over his work, his blond curly hair reflecting the light from the lone bulb hanging from a cord above him. Usually he had his green visor on to protect his eyes, but tonight he was bareheaded.

Even though the presses were quiet now, he didn't seem to hear the door open. The musty smell of papers and files greeted her. When Erik didn't look around, she closed the door even more quietly than she'd opened it, and tip-toed up behind him. When she slipped her arms around his neck and whispered, "Hello my darling," Erik jumped, gasped, and threw his pencil into the air all in the same movement.

"Heavens to Betsy!" he exclaimed in spite of her giggling. "Scare a person why don't you?"

Suddenly he had hold of her arms. Rolling back his chair he pulled her around and down into his lap. She was still laughing almost uncontrollably.

"Hasn't anyone ever told you not to sneak up on a fella who's been in the war? You might get hurt."

While his voice was serious, his blue eyes were dancing. "I have a good mind to..." But she smothered his words by pulling his head down and kissing him full on the mouth. As she had so many times in the past few months, she felt him melt in her arms. Never in her life had she been so happy as she was being Erik's wife. He constantly made her feel cherished and cared for.

"Now what was it you were going to do?" she teased.

"Mrs. Torsten when I'm kissed like that I forget pretty near everything."

With her arms still about his neck she craned around to look at the layout lying across the desk. "Pray tell what was it that held your interest so intently that you didn't even hear the door open?"

"A flyer-ad for Zofness Brothers. Thanks to your leg work and sales ability, we seem to be doing more business in printing flyers than we are in selling newspapers."

"You're not complaining are you?" Clarette hopped up from his lap and studied the layout work he'd done. Although both of them had previously worked on newspapers, neither had had firsthand knowledge of putting an entire newspaper together from the ground up. But working together, and with a little help from Erik's father, they'd learned quickly.

"No complaints from me. How could I have ever dreamed the Lord would give me such a great partner?" He reached out for her hand. "Someone willing to work right alongside me in a little half-baked weekly newspaper office."

"You don't mind that I'm not home tonight getting your supper ready for you?"

"Now that's a silly question." He stood and stretched the kinks out of his long legs.

"One that needs answering every so often."

Gently, Erik drew her into his arms. "I chose the perfect mate for me, Clarette."

"Even if I can't cook?"

"You can so cook."

"Not like your mother."

"I didn't marry my mother. And your cooking is getting better every day."

"If Dovey hadn't helped, I never would've known how to light the gas stove."

Erik chuckled. "Clarette, you can do anything you set your mind to do, whether it's learning to operate a stove, or garnering half the printing business in Bartlesville."

His remark brought the thought of creating a community theater back to her mind—along with Will Rogers' encouragement to do so. But she wasn't ready to share that with Erik just yet.

"Come on, let's go home," he said.

"Don't you have to finish the flyer?"

He shook his head as he stepped over to the coat rack to grab his hat. "I was just working on it to kill time till you got back."

They walked together through the back room past the presses where the air was heavy with the aromas of ink and metal. Clarette had come to love that smell, especially when the presses were hot and running full steam. While putting out their very own newspaper demanded hard work, still and yet, it gave a measure of satisfaction and fulfillment.

Erik opened the back door for her and led her to their Model T. "And how was the show? I assume you have the scoop."

"How can I have a scoop when the daily will have the story out tomorrow and we won't have ours out until Thursday?"

"And you probably gave all the good interview material to Joe Barber." He helped her up into the car, closed the door, then stuck his head inside and kissed her on her nose.

She waited until he had the car running before answering. "I sort of felt sorry for Joe. He was so nervous at meeting Mr. Rogers tonight I thought he was going to collapse. Can you imagine? With Will Rogers, the man who can make anyone at ease. Joe barely asked a question at all. Just took notes."

"Reaping all the benefits of your expert interview."

"I guess you could say that. He just needs someone to teach him the ropes."

After a moment he said, "Well, I guess we can consider it as seeds of good will planted for young Joe."

She gave a little sigh. "Exactly. That's exactly the way I felt about it."

Erik nodded and smiled. "I thought you would."

Her husband's sensitivity and understanding were unlike anything she'd ever experienced and therefore continually amazed her. "And the show was tremendous," she said returning to his first question. "The crowd went wild. Three or four curtain calls."

"Did he have a horse on stage?"

Clarette shook her head. "Not this time. He explained to Joe and me that he's traveling back and forth doing moving pictures in Hollywood and the *Follies* in New York. I don't believe a horse would fit in that hectic pace."

"And you'd seen his show at the *Follies*?"

"Several times. New Yorkers never get enough of that soft drawl."

"Did the show make you homesick for New York?"

Clarette glanced over at her husband, curious as to why he would ask such a question. "Now how could watching an old Oklahoma cowpoke make me miss New York? That doesn't make much sense."

"You know what I mean. Ever sorry you decided to marry me and came to live in this little out-of-the-way place? Ever wish you were back in the big city?"

Clarette worded her answer carefully, because there were times when she missed New York a great deal. Especially lately. Bartlesville was such a tight-knit little community, she wondered if she would ever fit in. But there was no way she was going to put that problem on Erik's head. It was something she and the Lord were working through. "Marrying you was the smartest thing I ever did, Erik Torsten." She scooted over close to him and snuggled against his side. "I'm happier than I've ever been in my life." And that was the truth!

To change the subject, she pulled her pad from her purse and read a few of the one-line jokes for which the humorist was so famous. They were laughing aloud as Erik pulled up in front of their small house on Chickasaw Avenue.

"What's all that racket over there?" came a high-pitched voice from next door. It was Dovey Clemmet sitting in her wicker rocker on the front porch.

"Dovey," Erik called out as he opened the car door for Clarette, "what in the world are you doing up so late?"

"Rhumatiz' acting up I s'pose." She rose slowly from the rocker, pressing her hand to her back as she did so, and walked over to the porch railing. A flour-sack print dress hung loosely on her thin frame; her black, fringed shoulder shawl snugged up around her neck kept off the chill of the early spring evening. "Anyway, cain't sleep like I used to in my younger days. Seems I sleep when I need to be awake, and I'm wide awake when it's time to sleep."

Clarette chuckled. In spite of Dovey's seeming complaining, Clarette knew her elderly neighbor was full of praise to the Lord for everything. Dovey's devotion to God reminded Clarette of her Grandmother Vanderpool back in New York—the only member of her family who'd ever talked to her about serving the Lord.

"Now what've you two kids been up to that's kept you out so late?"

"I covered the Will Rogers show tonight," Clarette said, "and Erik was busy at the office."

"Oh my, that Rogers boy. Wish you could have seen Little Willie when he was younger. Such a rowdy little feller."

"Little Willie?" Clarette glanced up at her husband who was nodding. Evidently all the old timers in Indian Territory had known about the Rogers family.

"I was friends with his sweet Mama, Mary. A Godly woman, too. The beautiful thing died so young. Willie was never the same after that. But now, just look at him cutting a fine figure in all them high-toned places."

Clarette felt Erik tapping gently on her arm. She knew he was concerned that Dovey might start delving into memories and not know when to quit. Which she did quite often.

"You would have loved the show, Dovey. Wish I could have bought you a ticket," Clarette told her. Then she quickly added, "By the way, is it all right to come over and use the Maytag in the morning?"

"Why, it surely is. You just come on over soon as you get ready. I'll have it out and ready. Might have a few things to throw in there myself."

Doing the laundry with Dovey's electric wringer washer was a far cry from doing it by hand which she'd done when they first arrived in Bartlesville. She and Erik lived in a small apartment above the hardware store on Keeler Street back then.

Clarette met Dovey at First Church where she and Erik attended. It was Dovey who'd told them of the vacant house for rent next door to her. The day they moved their few possessions into the little house, Dovey was at their door with a pot of split-pea soup and a basket full of cornbread. The friendship of this elderly neighbor had been a godsend for Clarette, who knew little or nothing about managing a household.

In the months since she'd been married, Clarette found herself wishing she'd taken trips to the basement laundry room of the Vanderpool mansion to take a few lessons. But when she was growing up, laundry was the last thing on her mind. Even after leaving home and living on her own, she'd sent her laundry out to be done.

Erik's tugged at her arm. "Good night, Dovey," he was saying, as he guided Clarette away from their neighbor's porch and around to their back door.

"Good night children. See you in the morning, Clarette."

"Good night, Dovey," Clarette called back.

"Children," Erik muttered softly to Clarette as he went up the back steps to open the door. "Don't you love that? She calls us children."

"To her we are. She probably has grandkids older than we are."

"Could be. Say, what's this?" Erik stepped across the kitchen to the breakfast table and picked up a slip of paper. "It's a note from Dovey." He held it up and read aloud, "*There're a couple pork chops in the icebox. They'll make a good snack before bedtime.*"

"That woman is a dream," Clarette said taking the note from Erik and studying the steady handwriting. "I truly believe God led us to live beside her." She laughed as she pulled off her hat. "Only God could know how desperately I was going to need her!"

Opening the icebox door, she took out a package wrapped in butcher paper. "They're all cooked," she said. "Shall I warm them in the skillet or do you want yours cold?"

"Cold is fine with me."

"Go wash up and I'll see what else I can put together."

Later when he came back dressed in his pajamas, robe and slippers, she had a nice little supper prepared of coffee, bread and butter, sliced cheese, apples, and of course, Dovey's tasty pork chops.

"I've never asked what you found out in Whizbang this afternoon." Clarette lifted the percolator from the stove and turned out the flame. Filling their cups, she asked, "Was it worth the trip?"

"I'm still not sure." He gave a wry grin. "I swear those boom towns never sleep. Rabble rousing goes on from dusk till dawn."

"Was it a murder?"

"Sit down and I'll tell you the gory details." After taking her hand and blessing the food, Erik explained about the murder in Whizbang which evidently had been spawned by a row over lack of sleeping quarters for all the roustabouts. "The violence is so common anymore, I'm not sure the people of our community are interested in that kind of news. What do you think?"

Stirring her coffee thoughtfully, Clarette said, "I think I'm very thankful you decided to begin our paper here and not in one of the boom towns!"

Erik leaned back in his chair in mock surprise. "What's this I'm hearing from the courageous girl who tried to defy the entire Oklahoma Klan? And took a whip on her back to prove it?"

"Please don't remind me." Clarette shuddered at the memory of the nightmare event. "It was ten percent courage and ninety percent ignorance." She moved to refill Erik's coffee mug. "To answer your question, I'm not sure about your covering the boom towns for news. I've yet to figure out what these people want to read about."

"Ouch! That hits a little close to home."

"I'm sorry, Erik. It's just that we both try to read several national newspapers daily to glean out the news. Our news coverage is far and above anything our competition is doing, and we're still not building up a strong subscription base. I'm bewildered."

"It takes time, honey. We're still the new ones in town. It's not been a year yet. God blesses diligence and persistence."

"I know," she said sitting back down at the table, "but why does He take so long?"

"God's timing isn't our timing."

"But how do you know if He's telling us we've made a mistake?"

Erik's blue eyes grew intense. "Do *you* think we've made a mistake?"

The seriousness of his tone snapped her back into reality. "Oh no, darling. Of course not. But thank you for making me look deep inside and see for sure. I'm your wife and my place is to stand beside you and support you."

He reached out, took her hand, and gently pulled her into his lap. "But it's also to advise me and share your wisdom with me."

Clarette lay her head against his chest. "Sometimes I'm not sure I have any wisdom."

"You're a Christian now, Clarette. That means you have Godly wisdom which God supplies. *'Sound wisdom is laid up for the just,'* the Scripture says."

Clarette remembered when she first met Erik, how she recoiled at his Scripture-spouting. Now she appreciated his strong stand for the Lord.

"Well then," she said pulling away from him, "I think my wisdom from God—however much I have at this time—says we should forget about chasing around to all the boom towns. First of all it's dangerous, and secondly all the news is the same."

She stood to begin clearing the table. "Let's continue doing what we feel is important—that of giving our customers the best national news possible. And with the time saved in driving to Okesa and Whizbang and all points in between, we can work on wooing more customers. Maybe we can even think up a new marketing strategy."

"See there?" Erik jumped up and grabbed her around the waist nearly making her drop the dishes in her hands. "Now that's what I'm talking about. That's good sound wisdom. Let me grab a sheet of paper and pencil and let's brainstorm for marketing ideas."

"Great. There's plenty of paper on the desk. We can spread it out here on the table as soon as I get this all cleared."

A moment later, Erik called from the adjoining living room. "What's all this stuff laying beside your typewriter?"

Clarette swallowed. She thought she'd put it all away. "What's what stuff?" She turned to see him standing in the doorway with a stack of pages in his hands.

With a puzzled expression he said, "It looks like a play script."

Chapter 3

"Now it's you who has the wisdom." She feigned a nonchalant air. "That's exactly what it is. A play script."

"*Journey's End*," he read from the cover sheet. "You never told me you were writing a play."

"You never asked."

"Clarette..."

"All right, so I'm a paranoid writer. I was going to sit on it for a while. I'm not too sure what I'm doing in this area. A play is a long way from a news story."

He gave a nod, but she could tell he wasn't quite convinced. He seemed to be hurt that she hadn't shared this little detail of her life with him.

"Are you going to let me read it?" he asked, still holding the script as though it were some sort of courtroom evidence.

"Eventually."

"Well, I'm sure you've seen enough good plays to know what might work." He turned to put the script back where he found it.

Clarette dutifully wiped the oilcloth table cover, washed the few dishes and placed them on a towel to dry. Erik returned to the table with paper and pencil in hand and together they went over ideas for increasing their customer base for the *Courier*.

As they talked, Clarette couldn't help asking herself why she hadn't told Erik about the play. Was it because she had such lofty dreams for it? Was it because she was ashamed of her longing to have the play produced on Broadway? Was she afraid she would alienate him if he knew? None of it was very clear, but she knew it made her very uncomfortable.

By the time the gong clock sounded midnight, they had several workable ideas, and the subject of the play script had seemingly been shoved to the background.

"This is enough for now," Erik said, his ready smile once again beaming. "No more running all over the country for stories, unless we both agree it's a story that warrants our time and energy."

"Such as the case of the Indian girl who was murdered for her head-rights."

"Yeah, like that." He folded the pages and set them in the center of the table. "What time are you coming down to the office tomorrow?"

"I'll do the wash, and hang out the clothes. Then I'll write the story on Will Rogers and then I'll be there."

By their mutual agreement, Clarette spent mornings at home, and afternoons and evenings helping with the work at their little office. It had been in those stolen morning hours that she'd worked so hard on the play script.

As always before turning in, Erik read a portion of Scripture after which they prayed together. Clarette loved hearing her husband pray over her, and sometimes, when it wasn't so late, she liked to ask questions about the Scriptures and he patiently explained the answers.

Erik turned out the kitchen light and together they walked through their small living room to the back bedroom. They'd been married for nearly eight months and still their home had only a few pieces of furniture. The ivory-enamel steel bedstead had been a wedding gift from Erik's parents—along with the mattress and springs.

As Clarette went into the bathroom to scrub her face and brush her teeth, she heard a thud then a yowl from Erik.

With soap burning in her eyes she called out, "What is it Erik? What happened?"

"I stubbed my toe."

"On what?"

"This box!"

Uh oh. It was the boxed-up silver tea service, which was their wedding gift from her parents. Quickly she patted her face dry. She came to the door of the bathroom to see him sitting on the side of the bed rubbing his great toe. He looked up at her. "Did you have this out?"

She nodded sheepishly.

Erik flipped open the box to pull out one of the gleaming silver pieces.

"Why? Were you polishing it or wishing you could use it?"

"Silly man. Neither one." She sat down on the bed beside him and took the piece from him. "I grew up with this stuff everywhere. It means nothing except that you need hired help to keep it polished."

"Then why was it out?"

She pursed her lips. It seemed she now had two secrets. But this one was easier than the first. "If you must know, I was seriously considering selling the whole mess."

"Clarette, you can't do that."

"Why not? There're things we need, and all this is doing is..." She pointed to his toe. "Is waiting beneath the bed to sneak out and attack you."

"But this was a gift. You can't sell a gift."

"I can so. I don't think Mother and Father will be visiting any time soon; they'll never know the difference."

"Is that why the Sears, Roebuck catalogue was out?"

"You notice everything."

"It's not a very big house."

Clarette gave a little snicker. "Did you peek at the turned-down pages?"

He shook his head. "I didn't dare."

"I priced a chest of drawers and a davenport. I think the silver set might bring enough to cover both."

Erik put his arms around her and pulled her close. "I so wish I afford all those things for you, my darling."

The wistfulness in his voice made her heart ache. "I know that, Erik. But you have to realize that *things* don't mean much to me. I want the items I mentioned because we need them. Promise you'll let me sell the silver service and not get upset about it. Please?"

Reluctantly he agreed, and then added, "We might want to take it to Tulsa to check out the best prices there."

"Ah, a trip to Tulsa! I'd like that." She jumped up to finish getting ready for bed. At the bedroom door she paused and looked back at her strong, handsome husband. "Thank you for being so understanding."

In a few minutes she was snuggled up against his massive, muscular back, feeling contented and happy. However, just before falling asleep she thought again of Will Rogers' advice about starting a theater company right there in Bartlesville. She was shot through with fresh excitement at the possibility of that venture.

THE NEXT MORNING AFTER Erik left, Clarette lugged two basketloads of clothes to be laundered over to Dovey's back porch. The Maytag was already full of sudsy hot water. Dovey had taught her how to separate colored things from the lighter ones and to wash the lighter ones first.

Dovey's screened-in back porch held an interesting clutter of many things, from old fruit jars and cast-off newspapers, to a disarray of potted plants and skinny seedlings for her garden. Dovey had lived in Indian Territory since the 80s, having come there with her family following the Civil War. Many times Clarette had heard Dovey's stories of Jacob Bartles' grist mill and trading post located on the north side of the bend in the Caney River—the very first business establishments. Dovey could remember when the Nellie Johnstone well came in. "Oil spewing up and splattering all over ever'where," she'd say, chuckling to herself. "Before you knew it, there was oil wells all over town."

"Right in town?" Clarette had asked. She couldn't imagine oil wells inside the city limits.

"Mercy, my dear, they were ever'where! One was right smack in the middle of the street." She'd shake her head at the memories. "That's when the boom hit," she'd say. "People came into town by the scores. Harrington's Livery didn't even have enough hacks. Had to buy more!" Although Dovey's lively tales were repeated many times, Clarette never tired of hearing them.

She had the first batch of clothes in the Maytag and the agitator turned on by the time Dovey came out.

"Well, looka here, if it ain't the little housewife," she said as she pushed open the screen. In her hands she carried a metal tray holding two mugs of coffee and slices of cornbread lying on a blue china plate. "You're doing a mighty fine job there."

With Dovey's laundry stick, Clarette lifted pieces from the hot soapy water and guided them carefully through the wringer into the galvanized tub of rinse water. "Does that mean I'm a good student?"

"Willingness to learn makes a good student." Dovey set the tray on a low table next to her rocking chair. "And that fits you to a T."

Clarette laughed. "How about the necessity to learn?"

Dovey's toothless smile showed her amusement at the joke. "I've had to learn a good many things in my life out of necessity. Funny how life is." Slowly she lowered her thin frame into the rocker. "First I had to learn to care for a big family and a hungry hard-working husband. Now I'm trying to learn how to get along by myself."

Lifting the gear on the wringer, Clarette swung it around to wring out the clothes from the rinse water into the waiting laundry basket. "And *you're* willing to learn, right?"

"God asks us to be pliable clay in His hand, Clarette. And in the book of James it says that wisdom means we're easy to be entreated."

"Tell me what that means," Clarette insisted. Dovey was a life-long student of the Bible and Clarette wondered if she would ever learn half as much.

"Sit down and have a cup of coffee before you start the next load," Dovey said. "Then I'll give you a hand hanging them out."

"That's a tempting offer." Clarette wiped her hands off on an old towel she'd brought along, then sat on the floor beside Dovey's rocker. "Now about 'entreated.'"

"It's just what we were talking about. Easily taught. Pliable. Not wanting things our own way, but constantly seeking God's way. 'Yielding' is another way the Bible describes it."

Dovey laid her head back and closed her eyes as though she were thinking. "You know the story about Abraham and Sarah?"

"I know some—the part where God promised them a son when they were way past child-bearing age."

Dovey nodded. "That's the story. Abraham was yielded and full of faith. But by and by his faith got tired and so he took matters into his own hands."

"That's when the handmaid Hagar came into the picture?"

"You do know the story. You're exactly right. Ishmael was not the son of promise, Clarette. When we take matters into our own hands, when we try to *make* things happen, we make a mighty big mess of everything."

Clarette took a bite of Dovey's melt-in-your-mouth cornbread and washed it down with the strong coffee. "I never thought living the Christian life would be so hard. After I asked Jesus into my heart last summer I felt like I'd been scrubbed inside, just like those clothes there."

Dovey laughed. "Now that there's as fine a description as I ever heard."

"But I don't always feel that way."

"Don't have to feel that way all the time."

"I don't?"

"We get lots of good feelings along the way, but when they ain't there, God's still there. Just think, girl, of all the Christians everywhere. Would our great God twist Hisself around to fit their feelings?"

"No I guess not."

"Well, I guess not either." Her wrinkled blue-veined hand picked up another piece of cornbread which she chewed thoughtfully.

"Will you show me that verse in James later on?"

"Course I will. Now why don't you tell me all about the show last night while you finish that last load. First tell me who all was there?"

"Just about the whole town." Clarette rose and moved to place the last load in the Maytag and sprinkled in the washing powder. Over the sound of the chugging motor, she recited to Dovey who all was there in the special reserved boxes.

"I'm not surprised the Fosters were there," Dovey happened to remark. "I'm told Vernon Foster has a special love for theater."

"Really?" Clarette looked away from the wringer momentarily and when she did, one of the buttons on her best navy dress snapped in two as it went through the wrong way. Dovey had taught her to carefully fold the buttons to the inside so they wouldn't break in the wringer. Ignoring her momentary irritation, she asked, "How did you know that about Mr. Foster? I've never heard of him taking much interest in the theater here."

"He's too busy, no doubt. Besides that, he and the missus keep to themselves a good deal. I heard tell before he came to Indian Territory—when he still lived in Wisconsin—he played parts in a little theater there."

"You don't say."

"But that ain't the half."

"It's not?" Clarette was careful to keep her eyes on her work now, but to keep this conversation going.

"Marie—Mrs. Foster—was on stage herself."

"Drama?"

"Singing and dancing, I was told."

"She's certainly pretty enough." Clarette thought back to the well-dressed lovely lady with the dark eyes, sitting next to Mr. Foster in the box at the Oklah the evening before. Amazing that a former vaudeville actress should be married to the man who at one time held the largest oil lease in the country—and more amazing that both of them loved the theater. Clarette's plans, based on Will's suggestion, suddenly took a more definite shape.

Clarette went on to tell Dovey about who all attended the show, gave some of Will's quips from the show, and even told about the interview afterward.

"I knowed that boy when he was a youngun' tearing up the territory on that buckskin horse of his. Seems kinda odd that people are now pushing and shoving to grab a little glimpse of him."

"That's what fame can do," Clarette said. She picked up one basket of laundry and Dovey, after putting on her straw gardening hat, took the other. Clarette used to insist that Dovey not carry such a heavy load, but had long since ceased to argue with her. Dovey was still a strong lady, even if she was a little stiff in her joints.

They walked across the drive to Clarette's back yard where Erik had strung up a taut wire clothesline for her. As they hung the clothes up in the bright sunshine, Dovey asked, "Now you're planning to stay after church Sunday for the picnic aren't you."

Clarette rolled her eyes at the thought. The mention of church was a sore spot. Try as she might, after all these months, she'd struck out with the nice Christian ladies at First Church. In fact, the last few weeks, she'd simply stopped trying. She only attended because of Erik. Even Erik's mother, Lillian, hadn't come to her rescue. And while Erik's father, Arthur, was much more kind and thoughtful, he was out of town a great deal and attended church only on occasions.

"I'll lend a hand to help you fix up something real nice to take," Dovey went on politely just as though Clarette had answered.

"Thank you, Dovey. I'll certainly need your help. Nothing I'd stir up would suit anyone there."

Dovey whipped a pillowcase to shake out the wrinkles before pegging it to the line. "Now that's not so," she said.

"Oh, Dovey, I'm sorry. I'm speaking of your friends, and I'm very sorry." The struggle of trying to be nice was one she seldom conquered.

"These things take time, you know."

"Mmm," Clarette mumbled around a mouthful of clothespins.

"Yes I know." But she didn't really know. She felt they'd had plenty of time to accept her. The worst part was that she'd never figured out what they didn't like about her. Was it the fact that she had a college degree? Or that she'd worked on a New York newspaper? Or that she was published in national magazines? Or that she was now working and not staying home cooking and cleaning? Or perhaps they didn't like her New York accent. Whatever it was, she'd hit an impenetrable wall and she was weary of butting up against it.

"Happened during the boom, like I told you before," Dovey said, handing Clarette the opposite end of a bed sheet so they could stretch it on the line together.

"What happened during the boom?"

"Growing resentment of newcomers."

"Oh." That made a little sense.

"All them people... Why, it wasn't all nice, clean oilmen in business suits back then. It was every type of person comin' from everywhere who had oil fever. Some was just looking for work. Be that as it may, they made quite a mess of our neat little town. Bad feelings die hard, I suppose."

Clarette still couldn't see how that affected her. "So what do I do?" she asked.

"Just keep being as sweet as you are."

Clarette sighed as she took off her clothespin apron and dropped it in the empty basket. "I'll try. Really I will."

"You're doing fine." Dovey pulled off her hat and fanned her face. "Now I'd better get in out of this sun and rest a little while."

"Yes you should." Clarette stepped over to give her friend a hug. "Thank you so much for all your help."

"Pshaw. T'ain't nothing." The woman turned to go.

"Dovey, may I ask you one more thing?"

"You surely may."

Clarette wrestled with her thoughts for a moment wondering how to say what she wanted to say. "Is a wife supposed to tell her husband everything? I mean is it wrong to keep an idea for a while?"

"That all depends, my dear."

"Depends on what?"

"On a lot of things."

"Such as?"

"Such as how much that *idea* affects him. Such as asking yourself why you don't want him to know. That sort of thing."

"Did you ever keep things from your husband?"

"Can't rightly say I did. Seems he knew everything I did, and likewise me about him."

"Thanks, Dovey. I'll see you later." That pretty well answered her question, she thought as she stepped back inside the house and put her baskets away. She asked herself why she was reluctant to tell Erik about the idea of the theater. Now she realized—at least in part—it was because she thought he might be against the idea. She was so accustomed to launching headlong into her own projects with no approval from anyone. In fact, in years past, she'd taken on many things against her parents' wishes. But now that she was Mrs. Erik Torsten she no longer had that freedom. It was a difficult adjustment.

Common sense told her she needed to tell Erik about her exciting idea for opening a little theater in Bartlesville. And the longer she waited, the harder it would be to tell.

Chapter 4

F lies buzzed incessantly in an effort to push through the dirty plate glass windows that fronted the *Courier* office. Erik had his chair turned partially toward the door with his feet propped on the desk. The front door stood ajar allowing the warm spring breeze to waft in. He watched with detached interest as the flies flew wildly up and down the dusty windows. Those caught unawares in the long strips of sticky yellow flypaper buzzed louder than the others.

Erik felt a little like those flies this morning. Being confined indoors when spring had arrived proved difficult. The rugged, rock-strewn Osage hills were calling to him. Another few weeks and the dogwood and redbud would burst into bloom. His mind filled with fond recollections of long treks made with his father through those hills.

Adjusting his green-tinted visor, he smiled as he remembered the first time he took Clarette for a ride in the hills. They'd gone to Gray Feather's home for Clarette to interview him and get a story. Afterward they borrowed two of the old Osage Indian's mounts. For an Easterner, Clarette surprised him with her riding abilities and the way in which she maneuvered her horse through the narrow winding trails.

Locking his fingers behind his head, Erik stretched further back in his wooden desk chair. That day, when they waded in the cool streams together, was the very day he knew he wanted to marry the beautiful Clarette Fortier Vanderpool. The moment he held her in his arms and kissed her, he knew. And he'd never been sorry. Day after day, he marveled that he should be so blessed to have her as his very own. Now he hoped against hope that she wasn't sorry about her decision.

Suddenly he let his feet hit the floor with a dusty thud. He stood and strolled to the front door to watch the mix of morning traffic criss-crossing the intersection of Sixth and Jennings. Model Ts were interspersed with a few nicer Chevrolets, Packards, and Dodges. Some days there would come along a stretched-out, chauffeur-driven Pierce-Arrow limousine with an oil-rich Osage Indian seated proudly in the back. Today a couple of farm wagons pulled by mules sauntered by, their clopping hooves echoing on the brick-lined pavement. Across the street the welding company, kept constantly busy by oil field demands, was bustling with activity.

Erik thoughtfully leaned against the door frame mulling over Clarette's remark last evening about selling the silver set. Most women he knew loved those kinds of *pretties*. When the two of them moved from their crowded upstairs apartment to the house on Chickasaw, he'd encouraged her to set out the silver on the sideboard.

He remembered her chuckling at the suggestion. "Only if you agree to keep it polished," she told him, poking her finger playfully in his chest as she said it.

That ended the conversation. The box was kept under the bed. Personally, he looked forward to the time when they could have nicer things in their house.

Dejectedly he shook his head. Sometimes his wife was a bit of a puzzle. He was proud of the fact that she was willing to put in long hours with him at the *Courier* office. But what was this thing with writing a play?

Erik never seemed to shake the thought that Clarette wished she were back in New York. In his imagination he envisioned her carving out a niche for herself in that teeming city. He had no doubt his wife could do most anything she put her mind to, and he had no desire to quench her vibrant, lively spirit.

He turned back to his desk and forced himself to finish the layout. There were still two more printing estimates to figure. Where had the morning gone? Tonight they would print the paper and tomorrow it would be distributed around town and to their subscribers in the outlying areas.

In spite of their agreement that Clarette stay home in the mornings, Erik secretly preferred to have her by his side every moment. If she'd been in the office the past few hours, he'd have finished twice the amount of work. That's how she affected him. And even now, he marveled at how excited he became anticipating her cheery voice when she popped in the door with his lunch.

When the weather was bad he drove home to eat and gave her a ride to the office, but now that spring had arrived she wouldn't hear to that. "I need to get out and walk," she told him emphatically, "and there's no need wasting extra gasoline when I have two perfectly good legs."

"I agree to one part of that," came his answer. "The legs are good and perfect."

His comment made her laugh, but he remembered the warmth of her kiss in response.

Just then, the jangling phone startled him. And as though he'd called her to him through his thoughts, Clarette's voice was on the other end.

"I just pulled the Will Rogers article out of the typewriter and wanted to let you know the length. Thought it might save you some time rather than waiting till I got there."

"Thanks, sweetheart. I was hoping you were out the door to come this direction."

"Not yet. Remember this domesticated little housewife did the wash this morning."

He had forgotten. He didn't want to tell her that he wasn't even ready for her piece to be placed yet. He scribbled the word count, and mentally sized it to the front page. "What's left to do there?"

"Fix your lunch."

"Aw skip it. Let's just run down to Henry's for a sandwich. It's so nice out and I need a break."

"Erik, we have all the makings here for lunch. I already have the bologna out. We'll save those pennies for a special night out. Besides we don't have time today, of all days."

There it was again. The way she kept everything in perspective. "You're right. Bring on the sandwiches. But at least pack yours too and eat with me."

"That I can do."

Erik smiled as he hooked the receiver on the pedestal phone and forced himself to go back to work. He opted to stay with the layout and let Clarette do the price estimates. Now he was motivated to get it finished by the time she arrived. Miraculously he was putting on the finishing touches as she breezed in the door humming a little tune to herself.

She was dressed in her khaki knickerbockers, long socks and oxfords. Her white middy blouse, with the navy collar and ties, hung loosely over her slender hips. Of all her outfits, this was one of his favorites.

"Hi darling," she called out pulling off her felt-brimmed hat and shaking loose the curls of her short bob. She pecked his cheek before hanging up her hat and placing the shopping bag containing their lunch on the desk.

"Is that little kiss all I get after slaving in this office all morning, dying of neglect without you here?"

Her laughter filled the room and swept around him. "Crazy fellow." She handed him a sandwich wrapped in waxed paper and in the same motion gave him a more serious kiss.

"That's more like it," he said pulling an extra chair nearer the desk and guiding her to it.

"And what about me slaving over the hot wash water all morning?"

"Of course, you need a kiss for that, too."

Still laughing at him, she reached up to put her hands on his shoulders and pushed him down into his chair. "If you keep this up, we'll never even get through lunch, let alone all this work done around here."

As they ate she looked over the front page. "I'm glad you thought Will should be front page," she said, taking a bite out of an apple. "It's really more than entertainment, given that he's a home boy." She dug into the shopping bag, pulled out a folder and handed it to him. "This was such fun to write. What an easy personality to interview."

He took the folder and scanned her article as he ate. "No airs you mean?"

"No airs. Not like some of the people around here who have no reason at all to put on airs—but do so anyway."

Erik glanced up from the typed page. "What's that supposed to mean?" He could tell from her expression she was immediately sorry she'd even said it, but it was like a knife in his gut. He knew she'd had a difficult time fitting into the social structure of his home town.

"I'm sorry," she said handing him a boiled egg. "When will I ever learn to keep my big mouth shut?"

"If you don't speak out, how can I know what's going on inside you?" Then he chuckled. "As if I ever could. There's always so much going on inside you."

"Dovey tells me that time will take care of things."

"You've told Dovey something you haven't told me?" He salted his egg heavily and ate it in two bites.

"Woman-talk at the clothesline."

"About people putting on airs?" Erik couldn't figure out where this conversation was going, but almost immediately the stern face of widow Exa Belle Traeger popped into his mind. Even with her influential husband dead and gone, she still seemed to rule the church with an iron hand. He wondered what he was supposed to say to make everything all right for his wife. "Dovey reminded me about the potluck after church Sunday and I made a thoughtless and unkind remark."

He felt heat rising to his neck as he thought how the ladies clustered about each Sunday like so many clucking hens, and how his wife was kept outside the circle. Even his own mother was no help. Much as he loved her, her quiet personality would not allow her to confront people like Exa Belle. Sometimes he wondered if his own mother were ashamed of her new daughter-in-law. Well, what did it matter? Clarette didn't need them. She was better than the whole lot of them put together. He stood up, crumpling the pieces of waxed paper and tossing them into the nearby wire basket. Moving about might help him cool down. "We won't even stay for the dinner if you don't want to."

"Nonsense. Of course we'll stay for the dinner. Dovey's even promised to teach me how to bake popovers to take." She gathered the remains of their lunch and cleared the desk. "You know if she keeps on with her great lessons, I may one day be a pretty good cook."

Erik had a number of comments ready to burst out, but not one of them was fit to speak. How was Clarette ever supposed to grow as a Christian when Exa Belle and her ilk acted like hypocrites; but worse how would she grow if he spoke ill of them and passed judgment? Still and all, he wanted somehow to protect her from their cruel jibes.

Coming up behind her he put his arms around her tiny waist. "I wouldn't care if all you ever fed me was bologna sandwiches for the rest of my life. I'd still feel I was the luckiest fellow on this earth."

She reached up to pat his cheek. "Don't tempt me," she teased. "Now point me to the work. I suppose you've left the print estimates for me, right?"

He kissed the top of her brunette waves. "How did you guess?"

They worked amicably throughout the warm afternoon lost in their own thoughts. Periodically people would mosey in and out bringing last minute local news items, asking sheepishly if they were too late.

Erik always tried to please them as best he could, happy that the *Courier* was being recognized as a viable outlet for local news.

Clarette had whipped the estimates out in no time and was ready to help with the presses. Even in her quickness, he was sure she was closer on the money than he would have been. Every estimate he'd ever made he somehow cheated the *Courier*. "Too soft," Clarette would tease him. "You've got to learn to be more greedy." She was joking, because her estimates were never greedy—they were fair and reasonable.

Later as they were working at the press, she deftly fed in the slip sheets by hand as each page came off. Even dressed in her leather apron, and with ink smudges on her nose, to Erik, she was beautiful. She seemed deep in thought today. Probably dreading the upcoming social event on Sunday where she would once again be ostracized.

Suddenly Clarette surprised him by asking him if he knew much about the Foster family. The odd question took him off guard.

"Everyone in Bartlesville knows about the man who once held the million-acre Osage oil lease." He raised his voice to be heard over the clanking of the press. "But knowing *about* someone is a whole lot different than knowing them. Vernon Foster, I'm told, was educated back East, as well as in London, and he keeps pretty much to himself."

"And his wife?"

Erik looked at Clarette's bright dark eyes and wondered what was cooking in that head of hers. "Marie Foster, *I'm told...*" he repeated with emphasis, "would much prefer to be back in her beloved Chicago." He wanted to ask if Clarette would prefer to be back in her beloved New York, but he bit his tongue.

"Do you think they would talk to me?"

"Talk to you? You want to do a story on the Fosters?" This didn't sound like the news-hunting Clarette. All of Bartlesville wanted to write about the oil barons and peek inside their glorious mansions.

"I don't want to do a story." She smiled. "I want to ask them a favor."

Chapter 5

Clarette forced herself to concentrate on the slip sheets and not miss one. Her heart was beating wildly as she feigned an air of nonchalance. She'd been wondering all morning how she would broach this subject with Erik. Now she'd jumped in with both feet.

Back home at the Vanderpool estate in New Jersey, Clarette became adept at keeping up a masquerade, and her family seemed to never see through it. Her loving husband, on the other hand, was quite different. His ability to understand her was both comforting and unnerving. At times like this, it was more the latter. Now he seemed to be looking right through her. It made her wish she'd talked to him about her play script weeks ago.

"You'll be in good company in looking for favors from the Fosters," he commented as the last of the pages ran through. Quickly he inked the rollers to begin the last batch. "I suspect everyone within shouting distance is on their doorstep for favors. What was it you had in mind?" He held off re-starting the noisy press, waiting for her answer.

"Dovey tells me they both like the theater, so I thought perhaps I could interest them in underwriting a little theater for the community."

"A theater? We have a theater. What's wrong with the Oklah?"

"I'm talking about real theater, Erik, not a vaudeville stage. For serious drama."

"You need a different kind of stage for that?"

"Not a different kind of stage, but a different kind of personality behind it all. Jesse Overlees isn't interested in theater art, he's interested in making a dollar. The Fosters, and perhaps the Phillips, too, for that matter, would be interested in little theater as a community project."

Erik adjusted his sleeve protectors and gave her a wry smile. "The play you're working on—it wouldn't happen to be serious drama, would it?"

Clarette smiled back, relieved that he was catching on and didn't seem shocked. "It is."

"And a community theater would give you a place to produce the play? Am I right?"

"Yes, but not only me. This could be a place for other writers, along with novice actors and actresses to have a place to work and learn. This is much different than shipping in outside talent like Mr. Overlees does. A community theater would benefit everyone."

"You've thought this through quite thoroughly."

"Oh no I've not." She didn't want him to think she'd been planning and not sharing with him—even though she had. A little anyway. Guilt niggled at her as she told him about asking Will the night before for the name of a play producer in New York. And how Will made the initial suggestion about starting a local theater.

Clarette braced herself, expecting him to accuse her of going to Will before talking to him about the play, but he didn't. He just nodded as he made a few adjustments on the press. Then he said, "Let's get this noisy job done, then we'll talk."

Later, as they worked late into the night bundling the papers, they talked over the idea of such a community project.

"You've never said whether you thought the Fosters might be interested in assisting," she commented.

"That's because I haven't the faintest idea what he might say. He's always seemed a rather formidable person to me."

"I thought I'd start with Marie first. Dovey tells me she was a stage star before marrying Mr. Foster."

"I've heard that, too."

Clarette studied her husband's face. "You don't seem to be against the idea," she said.

"Actually, I was thinking of sending a note to Mr. Rogers, thanking him for presenting a way to keep my wife's heart and mind in Oklahoma."

She held the cord as he tied the last bundle and dropped it by the door where their hired newsboy would pick it up first thing in the morning.

"I'm sure he'd get a kick out of that. Ready for a cup of coffee?"

"More than ready."

As she took the pot from the hot plate and filled their mugs, Erik pulled off his visor and sleeve protectors. Buttoning his cuffs, he asked, "Tell me, have you considered what role you'll play in the community project? That is, if you can interest our local oil barons?"

She tried to hide her guilty smile as she untied her apron, folded it and placed it on the storage shelf. "Well, I admit, I hadn't exactly thought of being a sideline spectator."

"That's what I was afraid you were going to say. Of all the hours you put in here, how did you figure you'd fit this little extracurricular activity into your busy schedule?"

She shrugged as she dropped into the swivel chair at the desk. "I haven't even thought that far ahead. I just know it's something I'd like very much to do." Watching the steam curl up from her coffee mug, she added, "I have more than one play idea in my mind, Erik."

"Of that, my dear, I have no doubt."

How had she ever deserved such an understanding husband? Clarette studied the way the light from the hanging bulb played on his tangle of tawny curls, all mussed from wearing his visor. "How do you think I should make contact with them?" she asked.

He reached over and grabbed the stem of telephone and lifted it off the desk. "This is as good a way as any."

Clarette tried to think of how her own mother might react if someone called her out of the blue looking for money for a project. But she couldn't imagine that happening. On the contrary, her mother had always been out looking for projects in which to be involved, and to use great portions of the riches from the Vanderpool Silk industries. The situation here in Bartlesville, Oklahoma was a great deal different.

She nodded her agreement. "I think you're right. I'll give a call first thing in the morning."

Erik stood and reached out to take her hand and pull her to her feet. Her tired calves screamed in protest. "Come on, Mrs. Torsten. Let's get home and get some rest."

She rinsed out the cups while he locked up. On the short drive home, she scooted close beside him in the Model T, laying her head comfortably on his shoulder, once again praising the Lord for her wonderful husband.

———◈———

WHEN CLARETTE TELEPHONED the Foster residence the next morning, she was told that Marie Foster had just left for a shopping trip to Chicago and wouldn't be back for several days. Erik suggested she go ahead and call Jane Phillips, but Clarette didn't feel that was the route to take.

"I think I'm supposed to begin with the Fosters," she said. "From what I can tell they seem to be the trend-setters here. If they commit to the project, the others may follow." Clarette had seen that pattern often in the social circles in which she'd grown up.

Erik just shook his head. "You know more about all that than I do." But he didn't argue.

On Saturday Eric worked on a few small print jobs at the office, while Clarette spent the afternoon in Dovey's small kitchen learning to make light fluffy popovers. There wasn't all that much to whipping them up. The secret, she learned, was in the oven temperature.

"A whole lot easier on this here gas stove than on my old wood-burning Betsy that I had in the cabin when I was first married,"

Dovey said with a chuckle, wiping her hands on the tail of her long print apron.

While the popovers were rising high in the oven and turning a light golden brown, they set about mixing up the vanilla pudding in the top of the double-boiler. The sweet vanilla aroma filled the room as Clarette dutifully stirred the mixture while it thickened. Before meeting Dovey, Clarette had never even heard of a double-boiler. Now she knew to cook their breakfast oatmeal in the top of the double boiler to prevent it from sticking to the pan.

By the time the popovers came out of the oven, the pudding had thickened and was making soft plopping noises as it bubbled in the pan. Together they sat at Dovey's kitchen table where Dovey taught her how to cut open the popovers and fill each one with spoonfuls of the smooth pudding and replace the tops.

As they worked, Dovey, as usual, fell into telling stories about her early days in the Territory and Clarette listened with rapt attention. At this point, it was much more pleasurable to think about the past than to look forward to the social event coming up the next day.

When two-dozen filled popovers were lined on a tray in the center of the table, Dovey served coffee in her nice china cups. They each ate a popover which Dovey had placed aside especially for the two of them. "To the victor go the spoils," she said, giving a funny salute with her cup. "Your reward for a job well done."

Biting into the light-as-air pastry, Clarette had to agree. It was a job well done. "I'll have a time keeping Erik out of these tonight."

"Promise him you'll make another batch for him next week," came the wise reply.

"Why of course, Dovey." She thought of whipping up a batch of popovers all by herself in her own kitchen. What a great feeling of accomplishment that would be.

Later, as Clarette took the tray and prepared to leave, Dovey said, "Now mind you, don't wrap these tonight or they'll weep."

"Weep?"

"Draw moisture," Dovey told her. "Just lay a tea towel lightly over them and they'll be ready to go in the morning."

They walked together onto the back porch. The Maytag wringer was pushed up against the wall, with the galvanized tub resting upside down on the wringer. Clarette glanced out at the skies which had grown cloudy throughout the afternoon. "Will the church dinner be indoors if it rains?"

"The men already have the tables set up outside. But Reverend Dabney said if it does rain, we can move them all inside to the basement quickly."

From what Clarette had seen of Reverend Dabney, she figured such a decision was probably near the extent of his decision-making abilities. As quickly as the thought formed in her mind, she chided herself for such judgmental attitude. She was struggling to learn to be fair and loving, even in her thought life.

"Thanks again for all your help, Dovey." She went down the back steps, balancing the tray carefully. "Now that I monopolized your afternoon, what are you going to fix to take to the dinner?"

"Oh honey," she said with a wave of her thin hand, "I already have noodles drying on the breadboard in the pantry. I'll get up early in the morning and have a pot of chicken and noodles thrown together in no time."

Clarette nodded, almost envious of her neighbor's ability. One part of her wanted to be able to cook like Dovey, another part of her wanted to work constantly on her play script—which was growing by several pages each day.

Entering her own back door, Clarette's thoughts turned again to their pastor, the Reverend Otis Bascom Dabney. He was a slightly built man with receding gray hair and a plain face. A face which, in Clarette's opinion, had very little character.

If she'd known when they first arrived in Bartlesville what she knew now, she would've insisted she and Erik attend another church altogether. But he felt they should attend where his family had attended in years past—where he'd attended Sunday School at a boy. But what did she know? She'd only been a Christian for a few short weeks.

The kitchen clock told her she had about an hour before Erik arrived home for supper. She rummaged through the icebox and found leftover roast. Perhaps she could cook a pot of hash like Dovey had taught her.

As she peeled and cut up carrots and potatoes and dropped them in the hot broth to boil, she thought back to the times she'd been with Preacher Sam and his wife Mama Sue in Tulsa. When Preacher Sam presented the gospel, it made the hairs on Clarette's arms stand on end. In fact, when the black folks in Preacher Sam's church prayed together, it was an earth-shaking event. When she tried to share her thoughts with Erik, he simply told her she wasn't to base her faith on her feelings.

The only other preacher she'd been around very much was Pastor Stedman who was a friend of Erik's cousin, Tessa. And while she'd never heard him preach, she could tell the first time she met him that he was a clear-thinking, decisive person. Pastor Stedman had light in his laughing eyes, while Reverend Dabney's eyes were dull and lifeless.

Lifting the lid on the boiling pot, a rush of steam scalded her wrist making her drop the lid with a bang. She bit her tongue before a word slipped out.

"Steam burns as bad as fire," Dovey had instructed her a few weeks ago. Pulling a mitt from the cupboard drawer, she tried again. At the touch of her cooking fork, the vegetables fell apart, and she proceeded to thicken the broth and add the diced meat. By the time she heard the putter of the Model T in the drive, the hash was ready. Mission accomplished.

Secretly, she knew the biggest accomplishment had been resisting the temptation to spend the last hour at the typewriter.

Chapter 6

As Clarette made up the bed on Sunday morning, she glanced at Erik standing before the bathroom mirror brushing back his unruly blond curls, and adding a touch of Hair Slik to compel them to stay in place. His height forced him to duck just a bit to see himself. The mirrored medicine cabinet had no doubt been hung for the person of average height, not a giant like her husband. She smiled to herself at how her love for him had grown the past few months beyond anything she could have ever imagined.

Smoothing the last of the wrinkles out of the lavender chenille bedspread she turned to pull her hat box from the shelf in the closet. She had argued with herself whether or not to wear her new dress which had been a birthday gift from Grandmother Vanderpool.

"I purchased this little spring number in the off season," came the neatly penned note tucked inside the package that had arrived in the cold of January. "A real bargain."

It was a joke between the two of them. Her grandmother's wealth would allow her to purchase an entire department store if she wished, and she had access to many of the frocks manufactured by her son's textile businesses as well. But Grandmother Vanderpool loved nothing better than to shop Fifth Avenue for the best bargain-basement markdowns. To her it was a game.

As Clarette firmed the hat on her cropped curls, she turned to study the queen-blue silk crepe. The contrast of white pleated jabot and cuffs made the blue more vivid. A double tier of pleated flounce on the skirt created a chic look that was purely New York. She touched the belt at the dropped waist and marveled at the workmanship and design. Few if any shops in Bartlesville would carry such a dress. Now she wondered if it were too much for First Church in Bartlesville.

Suddenly Erik appeared behind her and slipped his arms about her waist. "You look stunning, Mrs. Torsten. More than stunning. Elegant is a better word."

She placed her small hands on his wide ones. "I'm glad you like it."

"I'm not talking about an *it*; I'm talking about you." His blue eyes twinkled.

She turned to look up at him. "Silly, I knew what you meant. But my mind is on the dress. Do you think it's too much?"

"Too much what?"

Laughing she stood on tiptoe to kiss his cheek. "You're impossible. You know what I mean."

"My wife's a knockout. I'm so proud of her I'm about to bust all the buttons off this shirt, and you're asking me to be objective about whether the dress is too much for the occasion? I think you're asking the wrong person, my dear. Come on." He gently led her out the bedroom door. "Let's load up those scrumptious popovers and get going or we'll be late."

Clarette hurried next door to help Dovey out with her steaming pot of chicken and noodles while Erik fired up the Model T. They packed Dovey's dinnerware in the picnic basket with their own. After they were underway, Erik quipped about stopping along the way to have lunch. "I tell you, Dovey, that smells so good I don't think I can wait till afternoon to eat. I'm hoping Reverend Dabney preaches a short sermon."

"Never fear," she retorted. "I've never known the man to get carried away. He's almost as punctual as the Santa Fe when it comes chugging into town."

Clarette wanted to ask Dovey more about her thoughts on this pastor, but she refrained. Sometime when they were alone, she'd ask more. Perhaps her own thinking about the man hadn't been all that out of line. And she didn't miss the fact that Erik smiled at the comment.

The cloudless azure skies guaranteed that the dinner would be outside. Recent warm days had brought forth greening lawns, a few early lemon-yellow jonquils, and the barest hint of green in the trees. In spite of the picture-perfect day, Clarette's insides were churning. Each Sunday she dreaded going to church a little bit more than the week before.

As they drove past the two-story white-frame Foster residence on Johnstone Street, Clarette noted the flower gardens in early stages of cultivation. She marveled at how modest the home was in comparison to the colonnaded Phillip's mansion over on Cherokee Street. Vernon Foster, Dovey had told her, was a Quaker and cared very little for the trappings of wealth. That fact alone made Clarette know she'd like this family very much.

Thinking about her proposed visit with them, and about the exciting prospect of being involved in a little theater, helped soften her dread of the afternoon.

As usual, Erik's father was out of town. This time he was in Ponca City helping protect the head rights for the Osage Indians. When Arthur and Erik were both at church with her, Clarette was ever so much more comfortable. Arthur Torsten was a gentle soul, whose sensitivity won Clarette over from their very first meeting.

Erik's mother, Lillian, was as wavering as a willow in the wind. Clarette quickly learned that her mother-in-law fell in with whatever opinion she'd heard most recently.

The modest stone church, located a few doors down from City Hall was bustling with chattering adults and laughing children, all of whom were toting pots, pans, and covered dishes full of food, and baskets full of picnic supplies. Long planks placed across wooden saw horses created makeshift tables which the ladies had then covered with bed sheets. The food was being arranged by those of the Women's Society, a group that Clarette had avoided joining. Her excuse was her busy schedule working alongside her husband each day.

Due to Clarette's sales work about town, she was on first-name basis with more of the businessmen than she was with their wives. Several men greeted her now, commenting on her well-written Will Rogers article, or other tidbits of local news. As she stopped to chat, she could feel the glances from the women at the tables.

Erik must have sensed them too and he pushed her along. "Let's get these things set down," he said. "Sunday School is about to start."

Clarette found she enjoyed Sunday School class much more than church. The lessons intrigued her, and she was allowed to ask questions. Mr. Cooper, who ran the hardware store downtown, was an excellent teacher and took his role seriously. Each Sunday he gave Clarette something new to think about.

Church service, on the other hand, was something she merely endured. Coming upstairs following Sunday School, Erik guided Clarette to their pew midway down on the right side. Presently, Lillian came in and joined them. Sitting primly beside Clarette, she leaned over and whispered, "You look so pretty. Is that a new dress?"

Clarette nodded.

"Did you bring it from New York?"

Although a few women were still filtering in from outside, Reverend Dabney stepped to the pulpit to begin the service. "Turn to page four-thirty-eight in your hymnals," he instructed. "Let's all stand and sing together."

As Clarette reached for the hymnbook in the back of the pew, she answered Mother Torsten. "The dress is a gift from my family."

Lillian nodded as though that made everything all right.

As she sang, Clarette stared out the windows at the long tables out back. The food was now protected under a patchwork of colorful tablecloths and large bedsheets, fairly glowing beneath the bright sunshine. How she wished she could shake the feelings of not wanting to be at that dinner.

Across the aisle and down a bit, Exa Belle Traeger, glanced back, raised her brows then pulled her glasses off as though to get a better look. She nodded then, causing her black wedding-cake-shaped hat to bob. Clarette hadn't seen such a hat in years. It looked like something her own mother might have created in her millinery shop before the turn of the century. Clarette nodded back and offered a weak smile.

Exa Belle was a hefty woman with work-worn hands and gray-streaked hair, which she piled grandly atop her head. Looking at her broad shoulders, Clarette imagined the woman could have settled the entire Indian Territory single-handedly.

Because of Reverend Otis Dabney's monotone voice, Clarette's thoughts kept straying. Even the most boring professors at Columbia University had held her attention better than this man of the cloth. Her small Bible, another gift from Grandmother Vanderpool was tucked into her handbag. But seldom was there need to bring it out. Reverend Dabney seemed more intent on condemning the social ills of the nation than on applying God's word.

True to Dovey's prediction, the sermon concluded at precisely twelve o'clock. Reverend Dabney invited all to stay for the meal—"whether you brought anything or not," he said. "If you're a visitor, you're more than welcome to join us." After blessing the meal and pronouncing a benediction, he dismissed the group to the waiting food.

"You're going to help serve, aren't you, Mrs. Torsten?" Exa Belle asked pointedly as they strolled out into the warm sunshine

Clarette glanced up at Erik in question.

"You go on," he said. "I've been looking for an opportunity to talk with Slim Farnsworth. Now's my chance." And just like that, he left her to her fate.

They stationed Clarette at the cooler of lemonade where she filled cups and tumblers as members came by. She took special care not to drip any on her silk dress. The sight of plates heaped with good food made her mouth water.

Mr. Wallenger and Mr. Cramer, both of whom were *Courier* clients, stopped to chat with her before moving on through the line, as did several other of the town business owners.

Exa Belle in her usual form, bustled about giving orders like an Army sergeant. Every time Clarette glanced in her direction, the church matriarch was watching her. How she wished she could grab her plate and go sit down in an out-of-the-way spot. The line was still moving, however, so she obediently manned her post.

Lillian was working nearby, cutting all the pies and cakes. Presently, Exa Belle came up to see that the job was being done correctly. "Excellent, Lillian," she exclaimed. "What a nice job you're doing here." She moved the cakes which were already cut, away from in front of Lillian and situated the un-cut ones in closer proximity. "Just a little bit more, girls," she said to the servers with a wave of her arm, "then we can go through the line as well."

Exa Belle reached up to firm her hat as a little breeze picked up. "It's so good to see you making yourself right at home, Mrs. Torsten."

Clarette was unaware the comment was addressed to her until the stout woman was standing right beside her.

"I said," she repeated with a bit more volume. "It's so good to see that you feel right at home here."

The vague comment didn't seem to require a response, so Clarette politely nodded as she drew up another dipper full of lemonade and filled an outstretched cup.

"Not only here at church, but in the community as well." Turning to Lillian she said, "She's done well, don't you think, Lillian? Getting to know so many of the businessmen in town."

No one could miss the emphasis on the word *men*. Lillian mumbled her agreement.

"I was just saying to Grace Murdock," Exa Belle continued, "how all the men seem to sit up and take notice. Don't you think so too, Lillian?"

This time Lillian was more on the defensive. "Her work does take her all over town." Her voice was still soft, and she didn't look up from cutting the magnificent lemon meringue pie in front of her.

"My my yes," Exa Belle picked up on the comment. "All over town is right. I've seen that. But then, it must take a great deal of work to pay for such a classy crepe frock. Something pretty as this is sure to catch the eye of every fella in the place." Exa Belle was close enough to reach out and touch the white pleated cuff on Clarette's sleeve.

Clarette bit her lip and kept cool as she filled another cup. The woman's intent was obvious since several families coming through the line were within earshot. And it wasn't the first time Clarette had been the brunt of this woman's tongue.

"I've never seen anything quite like this in a store in Bartlesville," she went on, not bothering to lower her voice. "Must've cost a fortune. Never knew a newspaper to bring in much money. It's no wonder your husband stays in that office till late every night. Poor man must work himself half to death to pay for your nice little things."

Under her breath, Clarette was asking the Lord how much of this she was supposed to stomach, when suddenly Dovey appeared out of nowhere. "Exa Belle, did you know some of the children are running in and out of the church with their food? Why that foyer floor that you mopped last week is gonna be a purity mess if you don't get in there and put a stop to it."

"My word!" Exa Belle removed her glasses and let them dangle from the black velvet ribbon fastened to her ample bosom. "Why is everything always left up to me? Can't the parents take care of those little ruffians?" With that she turned on her heel and was gone.

Gently, Dovey took the dipper from Clarette's hand. "I'm finished with my dinner. I'll take over here. You get your plate filled and go eat."

Clarette could have kissed her. "Thank you, Dovey. Thanks so very much."

"Think nothing of it. Get on now."

Suddenly the food didn't look as appetizing as before. Hurriedly she grabbed a piece of fried chicken and a helping of potato salad and went to where Erik had their blanket spread out on the grass. Erik, however, was off playing a game of horseshoes with the men.

As she ate alone, she was reminded of the garden party at the Vanderpool estate which she had attended just before receiving her assignment to come to Oklahoma. It was her father's birthday party and it should have been a happy event, but it only served to show her that she didn't fit in that scene. Years earlier she'd removed herself from her family to work her way through school and then make it as a newspaper reporter. Now here she was, a Christian with Jesus in her heart, eating dinner with church folk in Oklahoma. But somehow she didn't fit here either. This was Erik's church, and she should be doing everything possible to be a part of it, but she wasn't sure what she should do. And she wasn't sure anything she did would ever be enough.

Who am I Lord and what do you want of me? Where do I fit?

Chapter 7

The opportunity to discuss the subject of Exa Belle with Dovey never materialized. She searched her mind for a way to ask her friend about Sunday's incident, but rehearsing it over in her mind it sounded petty and nitpicking. The only reason she cared anything at all about what Exa Belle Traeger thought, was because of Erik. She wanted him to be proud of her. After a couple weeks had passed following the church picnic, Clarette was sure she'd only imagined that there was any malicious intent on the part of Exa Belle. After all, the woman seemed to talk about everyone and everything.

The play script was progressing nicely. One evening she even had the chance to share the gist of *Journey's End* with Erik, explaining that it centered around a young man returning from war—how his life and his world was forever altered. To her surprise, he liked the idea.

After that, he was kind enough to ask each day how it was progressing. That's when she realized how silly she'd been to keep it from him in the first place. She was unaccustomed to having such support and encouragement.

Recent letters from her father indicated he was coming to grips with her marriage and her choice of a place to live. She'd sent him copies of the *Courier* when one of her better stories was featured. While he wasn't openly complimentary, he at least commended her on her ability to produce under such "dire circumstances."

Her mother, on the other hand, was still not talking much. Clarette's brother was married last Christmas, and of course Clarette was not there, which made her mother even more upset. Brother Aubert's wedding was proper and in line with what was expected of a Vanderpool—which meant marrying within the same social strata. Clarette shuddered at the thought.

Each night as she and Erik read Scriptures and prayed together, her prayers were nearly always ones of thanksgiving. Grandmother Vanderpool had told her that her steps were ordered of the Lord, and how right she was. The Lord had led her right to Tulsa, and right into the arms of Erik Torsten. Now she couldn't imagine her life without him.

———●———

THE MORNING CLARETTE learned that Marie Foster had arrived back in Bartlesville, she prepared to place a call to set up an appointment. Thoughtful Erik had moved Clarette's writing desk nearer the living room windows so she could gaze out at the greening back yard while writing. The soft April morning sent a gentle breeze through the open windows, billowing the Nottingham lace curtains. She paused a moment now to say a simple prayer before picking up the telephone.

The voice on the other end of the line was congenial and kind. Clarette was surprised that the call went through so easily. She'd assumed the quiet lady would be less accessible. Knowing that it was best to be direct, Clarette came right to the point explaining the reason for wanting an appointment.

"While we do have a theater in town," Clarette said, choosing her words carefully, "it's of little good to the citizens except as a place to be entertained and a place to spend money."

She paused a moment waiting for a response. When there was barely an "Hmm uhmn," she continued. "A little theater presents the best of both worlds. The public can still pay to be entertained, but our own theater will incorporate local talent as the playwrights, actors, actresses, and stage hands. We can even design and build our own props."

"I'm familiar with little theater," Marie replied. "My husband was involved in one when he lived in Wisconsin before we were married."

Clarette smiled to herself. Dovey's information about the local oil man had been correct. She moved further with caution. "May I impose upon your time to talk further about the possibility of such a community project?"

"Have you talked to others in town about this?" Marie wanted to know.

Clarette was pleased she could answer with an honest, "No I haven't."

"I believe you should talk to my husband as well," Marie said. "Let me discuss it with our secretary. Vernon is out of town much of the time. When we find a suitable time, I'll have our secretary telephone you."

"Thank you, Mrs. Foster. I look forward to hearing back from you." Before closing the conversation, Clarette gave Marie both her number at the house and at the *Courier* office.

As she set the telephone back down on the desk, she heaved a sigh of relief. First step was taken. She was sure the financial backing was available in the city, but it would take time and effort to put it into action.

That done, she had almost an hour to work on her script before leaving for the office. Before she could roll a fresh sheet of copy paper into her Underwood, the phone rang. It was Erik.

"Dad just called from Pawhuska. He said the lease bids are going wild."

Clarette had often heard her father-in-law talk about the open-air bid sessions outside the stone courthouse in Pawhuska. Arthur Torsten assisted the auctioneer, all the while looking out for the best interests of his friends, the Osage Indians.

"You feel you should go up there?" She knew he did, but he needed to say it. This meant she'd have to leave to go to the office right away.

"We probably need to cover it." There was a pause. "I suppose a reporter from the *Magnet* is already there."

"If it's only Joe, you don't need to worry," she joked. But she knew even Joe could easily get a scoop on this story. She also knew what Erik was thinking—once again, he was wishing the *Courier* were daily and not weekly.

"Whether it's Joe or not, their story will be on the front page in the morning..." he said, confirming her hunch.

"We'll get there, Erik. Just you wait and see. Rome wasn't built in a day." She wished she had more than weak clichés to offer him. Quickly changing the painful subject, she said, "Please give Dad my best. Will you drive back tonight?"

"I plan to. But promise me you'll close up and go home before dark just in case I don't."

"I promise."

"If I decide to stay over, I'll call you."

"Thank you, darling. Bye." Hanging up the phone, she looked longingly at the typewriter for a moment. Perhaps there would be extra time that evening before Erik returned.

———◦———

GENTLY ROLLING PRAIRIES spread out on either side of the rutted, dusty road as Erik drove the Model T out of Bartlesville toward Pawhuska. The incessant transporting of oil equipment, rain or shine, had almost destroyed the roads throughout the Osage. Erik had seen trucks sunk in mud up past the axles—so deep it took teams of long-eared mules to pull them out. But nothing stopped the never-ending search for oil in this area.

Slowing the Model T, he pulled to the side of the narrow dirt road and turned off the motor. On the horizon he could see the towering derricks in the Whizbang field; the sounds of relentless pounding of drill bits were discernable in the still air. If he were standing outside, he would have been able to feel the vibrating pounding beneath his feet, even though the field was miles away. It was as though the very bowels of the earth were being disrupted.

Off in the opposite direction the thick blue stem grass flapped from blue to green as the wind shifted. Along a meandering creek clusters of short blackjack oak lined the banks, with a few taller cottonwoods interspersed in between. In spite of the flow of money and new business into the state, there were times when Erik almost hated what the oilmen were doing to this wild, beautiful land.

Allowing himself only a few moments of reflection, he again started the motor and drove on. Luckily, he encountered little oil field traffic along the way and the drive was relaxing. Winter browns were almost gone as the Osage hills were quickly greening under the bright Oklahoma spring sunshine.

Erik wasn't sure what made his father think this was a different day at the lease auction, but Arthur seemed to have a sixth sense about these things. Erik trusted that in his father.

Auction day meant Main Street in Pawhuska was a crazy traffic jam of automobiles, a goodly number of Indian wagons, along with dozens of horses and mules. When he arrived, tables had been set up by the Methodist women who were selling chicken dinners to the crowd.

He easily located his father who was sitting on a folding chair beneath the sprawling elm tree, eating his lunch and chatting with Colonel Edward Walters, the auctioneer. The Colonel, dressed in a bold, red-striped shirt and modified Stetson, knew these people well. It took a special type of person to be trusted by the oilmen and Indians alike, since the two entities were routinely at great odds with one another.

Clusters of Indians stood about with stoic expressions, dressed in colorful blankets draped over fancy silk shirts, wide beaded belts, and fringed leather leggings. Erik knew many of them by name. Some he'd gone hunting with as a boy. Although the Osage Nation was abundantly wealthy from oil money, many of these gentle people had little interest in wealth. It became a game to them to come into town and watch the white men fighting over the right to lease the land which the Indians held.

Arthur Torsten gave a hearty wave when he spotted Erik coming through the crowd. Pulling out his wallet, he handed a dollar to Erik. "The chicken's great. Here, take this and go grab a plate. My treat."

Erik smiled and took the bill from the older Torsten. His Dad probably knew he was a little short on cash. As he made his way through the lunch line, he recognized many of the regular faces of the oil men: the Phillips brothers, Frank and Waite, along with Skelly, Sinclair, Marland and others. Since the breakup of the Foster lease, Foster was also involved in bidding. However, Erik knew he never came personally, but sent a representative instead.

Plate filled, he returned to where his father was sitting. Around a mouthful of crispy fried chicken, he asked, "So what's up? Everything looks normal to me."

Arthur and Colonel Walters exchanged glances. "Just keep your pencil out and your ears open," the Colonel commented.

Erik gave another look around. "I don't see many reporters."

"Just the regulars," his dad said in his usual unruffled manner.

"Anyone here from the *Magnet*?" Erik wanted to know.

"I don't think so," came Arthur's reply.

Erik reached down to pick up his tin cup full of hot, strong coffee and took a sip. This might prove to be an interesting afternoon. Presently the Colonel excused himself, leaving Erik and his dad alone.

"So how's that lovely wife of yours?" Arthur wanted to know.

"She's at the office holding down the fort. Probably typesetting a few ads and flyers."

Arthur put his empty tin plate on the ground beside his chair. "She's quite a unique little lady, son. You're mighty blessed."

"You're telling me? Sometimes I have to stop and wonder if I'm dreaming. Did she really say yes? Was she really crazy enough to marry this Oklahoma boy?"

"Does she like it here?" his dad asked. "I mean, she's so talented, I was wondering if she..."

"Fits in? Is that what you're asking?" His father wasn't usually one to beat around the bush, but he was also extremely tactful.

Arthur pushed his hat back on his head and tilted his chair against the trunk of the elm. "You know how women get sometimes. I've seen how Widow Exa Belle looks down her nose at Clarette. Do they give her a hard time?"

Erik pulled apart a golden-brown cloverleaf roll appreciating the yeasty aroma as he considered the question. His father was expressing Erik's very own concerns. Sometimes he convinced himself it didn't matter to Clarette what others thought, but other times he wasn't so sure. "They make no effort to include her that's for sure."

Arthur nodded. "I thought as much. Lillian's not much help. Your mother's never been much of a trail blazer. No offense intended, just facts."

"I can't make 'em like Clarette," Erik said simply.

His father shook his head. "Nope you can't. But keep an eye out. Don't keep her roped in too tight. I don't think she's gonna be the mop-and-dustbin type."

Erik grinned. "You're right. She's in the middle of writing a play script right now. Pretty good one, too. She told me the plot the other day. About a man coming home from war."

"From what I've read of her writing, I figure she could write most anything she sets her mind to."

"She can *do* most anything she sets her mind to."

The older man chuckled to himself. Standing, he clapped his large hand on Erik's shoulder and gave a squeeze. "Just remember what I said. Don't keep her roped in too tight."

"I'll remember."

"And don't let the likes of Exa Belle have a chance to sink her claws in."

Erik nodded again. "I'll keep that in mind as well."

The rapping of the gavel by the Colonel interrupted the conversation. Erik watched as his broad-shouldered father strode off to go stand with his friends, the Osage, for the remainder of the bidding.

The afternoon bidding trundled along through the warmest part of the day with nothing out of the ordinary. During the quieter moments, Erik took Clarette's Graflex camera from the car and snapped a few photos. For what reason, he wasn't sure. He was beginning to wonder if he had wasted the day by driving all that way. However, just before suppertime, the air grew electric and the oil men were spring-coiled. Glances were exchanged and faces became grim.

Erik was familiar with the 160-acre patch being auctioned, and he thought it to be no different than all the rest. But then he wasn't an oil man. Suddenly without warning the bids had escalated to $900,000. No one had ever heard of such a price for a lease. An uneasy stillness fell over the crowd; even the children were subdued.

Colonel Walters, always the picture of cool decorum, held up a finger waiting for the bid to go to $920,000. He looked at Skelly; then at the Phillips brothers. Another bid came, then another. "I have one million dollars..." Walters shouted out as bedlam broke loose. Erik jumped up to run and find a phone to call Clarette. As he did the noise subsided, and he realized the gavel had not yet fallen. Frank Phillips had signaled Skelly and *together* they put the bid up one more time. When the gavel fell, the lease had been sold for over a million dollars. Strange events indeed.

Erik raced other reporters down the street toward the hotel and then he had to wait a few moments before a phone became free. None of the men were from the *Magnet*! When he reached Clarette, her voice was enveloped in static. She immediately wanted to know if something was wrong.

"Nothing's wrong, honey," he hollered through the waves of crackling static. "We have a scoop. We're going to put out a special edition with it tonight. Grab a pencil and take this down."

After several times of stopping, starting, and repeating, Clarette had the main details. "How about this for a headline?" he asked her. "*Giant deal made under the Million Dollar Elm.*"

"I like it," she answered. "Catchy phrase." He could tell she was writing as she talked.

"Clarette, you know more about millionaires that I do. Can you write an editorial for this?"

"The only millionaires I know have been that way for a lifetime; not overnight wonders," she answered. "But I'll think of something."

"I know you will."

Ringing off, Erik went back to thank his father before driving back to Bartlesville. The bidding was still going on, but nothing could top this.

"How'd you know?" Erik asked as he drew his father away from the crowd.

"Some things I hear; some things I sense."

"Which was this?"

Arthur winked. "Both."

"Thanks for the call. We're going to put out a special edition with the scoop."

His father smiled and nodded. "Good. Glad to be of help."

Driving back in the gathering dusk, Erik wondered if a few exclusives such as this might garner a substantial number of new customers. He'd always had a distaste for sensationalism, and yet that seemed to be what everyone wanted. And the *Courier* needed a boost of some sort. Without it, Erik seriously wondered if they would make it at all. A thought he tried to avoid as much as possible.

Chapter 8

Clarette was seated in front of the noisy clanking Linotype in the back room when she heard the front door open. In her excitement, she'd worked non-stop since Erik's call. She had the headlines typeset as well as most all the rest of the paper, leaving space for the breaking story and photos. Now she was finishing a couple of fillers waiting for his arrival.

"Hello!" he called out. "How's it going?"

One look at his beaming face made her even more excited. "Come look," she answered.

Pulling off his hat, Erik leaned down to kiss her. "What do you think of our scoop?"

"I don't think much of having so many aggressive oil barons in the state, but I'm glad you got the story."

Erik quickly scanned the type. Through necessity, he'd long ago learned how to read backward type. "Looks good. But what's this?" He leaned down for a closer look. "A report on church missions? What's that doing in our exclusive edition?"

Clarette had expected this initial reaction. "It's from Exa Belle."

"Was she in today?"

Clarette nodded and clanked out a few more letters on the Linotype. "She insisted we devote the front page to our church's new missions endeavor. 'After all,' she said to me, 'It's your church too. Aren't you proud of the work of your own church?'" Clarette parroted Exa Belle's grating voice.

"That woman has such gall."

"I told her I couldn't promise anything, and that I'd ask you. Then after you called, I began to think it'd make a pretty good juxtaposition."

"Church missions next to oil greed?" He hung his hat on the rack in the corner.

"Exactly. Plus the fact that I've pacified Exa Belle in the process."

Erik took down his green visor and twirled it on his forefinger. "Hmm. Not a bad thought. In fact, I think I like it." He reached down to tip up her chin and kissed her nose lightly. "But please keep in mind that you don't have to pacify the Widow Traeger."

Clarette turned back to her work. "You may not have to, my dear, but it seems I do."

Remembering his father's words, Erik shook his head. "Let's table the discussion of Exa Belle for another time. What say?"

"Agreed."

"Have you set the editorial?"

She shook her head. "I thought you'd better read it first. It's out there on the desk."

From the outer office, he called out, "Any coffee left?"

"Just made a fresh pot, and I even washed out your mug." She heard him laugh at her comment. It was an ongoing joke of whose job it was to wash dishes at the office. "Shall I develop the photos or will you have time?"

"You do that and I'll proof your editorial and set it."

"You know, Erik. I think we have a closeup of your famous auctioneer, Colonel Walters, in the morgue file."

He peeked back around the corner of the door frame. "Really? What a great memory you have. If you can find it, let's use that as well. That man is an incredible auctioneer."

Through the long night they worked side by side to finish the edition. He complimented her on the fine editorial. She complimented him on his great photos. Clarette telephoned their newsboys who were delighted at the opportunity for extra work. By dawn the boys were shouting from every Bartlesville street corner about the unbelievable transaction beneath the "Million Dollar Elm."

Erik scribbled a sign and hung it on the door saying, "Back at ten."

"Come on, honey," he said putting his arm around her shoulder and leading her out the door. "Let's go home and rest awhile."

———————◦———————

THE SCOOP WAS A WONDERFUL boost to their egos, but Clarette quickly realized from the ledgers that it wasn't going to make that big a dent in their finances. When she and Erik first rented their little office space and started up the *Courier*, she ordered a volume entitled *Bookkeeping Made Easy* for the sum total of sixty-nine cents from the Sears, Roebuck catalogue. Though she'd never been much good at numbers, she was determined to learn the double-entry bookkeeping system. And learn it she did.

Many times since, however, she wished she didn't know how narrow the margin of profit was. At times, it crossed her mind that perhaps neither of them was very adept as businessowners, but she dared not speak her thoughts. Erik seemed so determined to make a go of it.

———————◦———————

BY THE TIME CLARETTE received the call from the Foster secretary setting up her appointment with them in mid-April, her three-act play was completed. She felt it was perfect timing. She even dared to think that perhaps it was God's timing, but then she wasn't really sure about such things.

Periodically when she was alone, she made attempts at developing her private prayer life. Both Dovey and Erik had taught her much about prayer. But try as she might, she couldn't imagine God doing much of anything except frowning at her. Erik said it was probably because her own father was always doing just that. And probably he was right.

More than anything she wanted to see the little theater project underway, and she was confused as to how to pray about it. She couldn't say, "if it be Thy will..." What if it were not *His* will. Then what would she do?

When Clarette arrived at the Foster residence, she was greeted at the door by Marie herself, a gracious lady still possessing the poise of a professional dancer. Just as Clarette suspected, the Foster home was tastefully decorated, yet not flamboyant. An open stairway rose from the right of the wide entryway with an ornately carved grandfather clock tucked neatly into the far corner.

"Please, Mrs. Torsten, won't you come back to the sun room. My husband's waiting for us there."

She followed Marie through the sunken library, past a formal dining room and into the sunroom toward the rear of the house. The room was precisely designed to catch as much of the Oklahoma sun as possible. The louvered windows were cranked out wide to let in spring breezes. Cool chintz prints of matching designs covered the settee, the chairs and the plump pillows.

Vernon Foster, dressed in a lightweight cream-colored suit was sipping a glass of lemonade. He stood and reached across a low table laden with fresh flowers to shake her hand, while Marie politely made introductions. Mr. Foster was not a tall man, and his stocky build made him appear shorter than he actually was. He waved her to a chair and invited her to make herself at home.

Presently, an oriental lady stepped into the room to see what was needed. Clarette had often seen the young Japanese lady, named Sadako, here and there around town shopping for needed items for the Foster home. In only slightly flawed English, she inquired what Clarette would like.

"Lemonade's fine, thank you," she answered.

"Marie tells me you're interested in beginning a little theater in town," Vernon said, opening the conversation.

"That's right. I'm not sure how much I can do," Clarette told him, "but the first step seems to be to feel out the citizens and see if something like this is wanted."

"Vernon and I both agree that it's a wonderful idea," Marie put in. "The time seems to be perfect."

Clarette felt her hopes rising. "As you know I'm a reporter and my background is journalism, however, I'm interested in drama as well. Watching a performance is one thing, but being involved in a performance is a joy not many in our community are familiar with."

Marie leaned forward in her chaise. "I've been on the stage myself," she said, light coming into her dark eyes. "I know what you're talking about. It's an electrifying experience."

"Were you ever in drama?"

Marie shook her head. "Some musical comedy, but mostly song and dance. My sister and I were a team."

"I would have loved to have seen it."

"Here." Marie reached for a silver-framed photo on a nearby table. "This will give you some idea."

The two sisters, quite similar in looks, were posed in grand dresses of the '90s complete with mutton-leg sleeves and flowing skirts. Their smiling faces beamed beneath exquisite plumed chapeaus, all reminiscent of the Gibson-girl look of that era.

"They were highly talented," her husband added. "As a matter of fact, I fell in love with Marie from across the footlights!"

Clarette smiled at his remark, wondering how this quiet Quaker man had had the courage to court the lovely stage star. What a great story that would make.

Talk then moved to the actual work needed to begin such a community project. "I'll be more than pleased to help," Vernon told her, "but more than money is needed here. I'm sure you recognize that. It'll require the cooperation of the town—citizens and government alike. That's not always easy."

Clarette hadn't really thought that far ahead. Of course city hall would be involved. She wasn't at all sure how to go about it.

"I must tell you, however, that the Foster name is not be used in any way," he said glancing over at Marie. "We hold to a firm belief that good works are to be done in secret according to Scripture."

Clarette paused. She'd hoped to use his name to undergird the project and motivate others to give. Especially the other oil barons. This gave everything a different twist. "Would you be willing to speak in favor of the project to the mayor and council?"

Vernon shook his head. "Another principal I hold to is that I never visibly step into a political realm."

Another blow. Clarette attempted to mask her disapppointment. She should have already been aware of these facts, and yet she'd never really thought about it. Now as he spoke, she realized that Foster had been practically invisible compared to the others who'd struck it rich in the oil boom. Now what would she do?

"The ideal thing is to interest the citizens," Vernon went on, "and once they're behind it, I'll be pleased to match funds, and perhaps even double what's being raised by the community. Perhaps there'll even be a bond election to get it started. Either way, I'll help, but as I said, my name is never to be used."

So much for thinking she would open the Vernon Foster Bartlesville Little Theater.

Marie smoothed the skirt of her dress and clasped her hands around her knees. "You, Mrs. Torsten, are in a prime position to launch this project."

"What do you mean?"

"You have an entire newspaper at your disposal," she said with a dramatic wave of her hand.

Clarette thought about their tight fit for copy each week. "Well perhaps not an entire newspaper."

"Perhaps not, but even little notices can work wonders. I happen to know most people read every word of your paper."

The comment was flattering, but Clarette still wasn't sure.

Somehow she'd pictured the Fosters taking this idea and going forward with it. That's what her mother would have done. But these people were so content to remain invisible, as he put it. So different, yet so refreshing.

The conversation was winding down; it was time to go. Clarette stood and thanked them for their time and hospitality and the tasty lemonade. Graciously, Marie showed her to the door and bade her good-bye.

Out on the sidewalk, Clarette sucked in a deep breath. "Well, Clarette," she muttered, "it wasn't an out and out no, just a conditional yes. Time to keep moving forward."

Walking toward the *Courier* office, she wondered what the reaction of Frank Phillips might be. Pushing open the office door, she pulled off her hat, hung it on the rack and plopped unceremoniously into the wooden swivel chair.

"Well?" Erik said as he appeared from the back room.

Briefly she reported to him the response from the Fosters, then picked up the telephone to try to reach Mr. Phillips.

When Mr. Phillips' private secretary came on the line, Clarette introduced herself. "Why yes," came the polite voice, "I'm quite familiar with the *Courier*. Fine paper. Are you seeking an interview?"

"Well, no. I'd like to make an appointment with Mr. Phillips regarding a community project," Clarette pressed on.

"I'm sure you're aware there are many projects in which Mr. Phillips is already involved at the time. What did you have in mind?"

Briefly she outlined the plan for the community theater, then waited for the response. Getting past a secretary was seldom easy. "One moment, please," was the cool answer. However a few moments later,

Clarette found herself making an appointment with the secretary to see Mr. Frank Phillips in his office day after tomorrow.

Hooking the receiver in the cradle she looked up at Erik and grinned. "It may go yet," she said.

"Wouldn't surprise me a bit," he retorted, blue eyes twinkling. "You just have a way with people."

Clarette thought about that for a moment, wondering if it were really true. She didn't think for long, for Erik handed her a sheet of copy and asked her to being setting it.

Sitting before the huge formidable Linotype machine, which she only recently felt she had conquered, she patiently and carefully started the clink-clank of the machine to get the material typeset for the next edition. When she worked as a reporter for the *American*, she'd thought she was pretty savvy about newspaper work. What a far cry that was from running the whole show.

———◉———

VISITING WITH FRANK Phillips in his busy cluttered office, was quite different than her visit with the Fosters, and yet nonetheless productive. He too like the idea and felt his wife, Jane, would agree.

"We never miss an opportunity to see a Broadway show when we're in New York," he told her. "This would be like bringing a bit of New York to Oklahoma."

That, Clarette thought, summed up her feelings nicely. When he asked if anyone else were involved, she told him that a silent party had made an offer to be in a supportive role. She could tell by the look on his face, he knew she meant Foster.

"And what do you see as your own role in the project?" Frank asked her.

She had to stop and think a moment. This was something the Fosters had not asked. Just as well be up front and honest. "I've written a play which I'd very much like to see performed."

"I see." He studied her from behind his dark wire-rimmed glasses, his narrow face serious, but pleasant. "Did you also see yourself as a salaried executive director of the project?"

Now she was surprised. "No, I hadn't thought of that at all. Most of my time is taken helping my husband on the paper."

"Many times the best person for such a job is the one whose heart and passion is in the project," he said tapping a capped fountain pen on his desk.

She nodded. "That may be true, but that's not my ambition at all." Although it was an inviting thought.

Mr. Phillips went a step further than Foster and gave her a dollar amount above anything she could have imagined and offered to speak to the mayor and the city council.

Beaming, Clarette left his office on Third Street and nearly flew back to the *Courier*. As she walked along in the spring sunshine, in her head she was typesetting the headlines announcing the opening of the new Bartlesville Little Theater. And of course her play, *Journey's End*, was the featured opener.

Chapter 9

Nothing warmed Erik's heart more than seeing Clarette's excitement over the growing theater project. She'd taken on a new glow as she met with committees, sat in on the city council meetings and offered workable, concrete planning ideas. Pride welled up in him as he saw how much she was accomplishing.

As much as they could, they allowed spots in the paper for announcements and updates. By the time May rolled around, the project was enjoying strong community support. The only dark cloud on their personal horizon was cash flow. Or lack thereof.

Daily Erik struggled with the smallest monetary decisions. How much more should they sink into the paper? Their office rent along with payment for the bank loan, as well as the house rent, amounted to almost as much as they were taking in. Never in his wildest imaginations had he ever thought their little endeavor might not make it.

Late nights as they wearily drove home together, they discussed alternatives and fresh ideas. Should they plunge in deeper and go daily? Should they try for more printing jobs? Should they consider being the paper for several oil boom towns and forget about covering Bartlesville?

While Clarette seemed to be right on top of putting together the theater project, her thoughts on business endeavors were vague. "I've just never had to think in this vein before," she said. Her tone was so apologetic, it made his heart break.

She'd already given herself to his business venture with more gusto than he'd ever dreamed possible. Was he asking her to work in a realm that might be thwarting her talents? Repeatedly in the past few weeks, he thought of the remark his father had made—that Clarette was a multi-talented lady. As though Erik needed to be reminded.

How much should he ask of her? Was her heart really in this little paper? Then as his mind churned, he'd ask himself the most difficult question of all: was *his* heart really in the *Courier*? That's when he forced himself to shut out the thoughts altogether, for he could see no recourse.

————————●————————

ON THE FIRST SATURDAY of May a steady rain fell the entire day. Since March and April had been dry, most everyone in town was overjoyed that springs rains had arrived at long last.

Erik had stopped in the barbershop that morning for a haircut, and one of the men said he'd talked to a friend in Coffeyville, Kansas, who said it had been raining up that direction for two days. Heavy rain upstream, all the men knew from experience, could swell the Caney River in quick order.

That evening, Erik and Clarette put a printing job together in record time and arrived home at a decent hour. It felt good to be home snug and dry while the rain came pouring down outside. They'd no sooner cleared away the supper dishes when there was a knock at the front door. Most of the company they received knew to come to the back door. Erik went to see who it was.

There in the pouring rain, beneath large black umbrellas stood Exa Belle Traeger, Marion Duffendack, Wilma Bierly, and Pastor Dabney. Erik stared dumbly at them for a moment searching his mind. Nothing he could imagine would bring such a group to his door in fair weather. What could have brought them here in the pouring rain?

"Good evening, Erik," Reverend Dabney said stepping forward.

"Who is it?" Clarette was at his elbow looking past him. "Goodness sake, Erik. Have you forgotten your manners? Please invite our guests inside."

Erik sensed his wife's frustration as she bustled about taking coats and handing out towels, then scooted off to the kitchen to put on coffee. Erik followed her and grabbed kitchen chairs so everyone could sit down. As he did she shot him a questioning look. He raised his eyebrows and shrugged.

Several bland pleasantries were exchanged while Erik tried to swallow the growing anger in his throat. This was obviously not a social call.

"So tell me," he said, straining to keep his voice calm. "What brings you folks out on a night like this? Are you recruiting volunteers for the roof-repair committee?"

Wilma and Marion twittered. "You always did have such a good sense of humor, Erik," Marion said as she straightened her hat, then touched at her sleeves with the towel she'd been given.

Erik ignored the women and studied the face of the pastor instead. His eyes averted Erik's as he appeared to study the room. "Nice cozy home, Erik. Very nice," Reverend Dabney said with little emotion.

"You came out in the rain to see our home? We've lived here for several months."

"Yes, well, we've had a number of needy members recently. I find it most difficult to get around to see everyone."

"Except in a deluge?" Erik caught the pastor's expression then, and it was most troubled.

"See here," Exa Belle spoke up, "we've obviously come on church business. Why else would we all brave such a storm?"

"Then by all means," Erik said, "let's get down to business."

The noise of rattling cups and saucers came from the kitchen.

"Your wife should be present," Exa Belle said coolly.

Erik stood. "Her name is Clarette." He met Clarette at the kitchen door, taking the tray from her and setting it on the desk. He proceeded to assist her in serving the coffee. He could see she was embarrassed that there was nothing else to serve and he hurt for her. If it hadn't been raining so hard, he would have run next door to Dovey's for cake or shortbread. She always had something.

Soon they were seated and Wilma and Marion exchanged sidelong glances as a moment of uncomfortable silence passed. "Reverend Dabney? Are you going to address this situation or shall I?" Exa Belle asked.

The pastor straightened his back and spoke. "It's come to our attention, Mrs. Torsten, that there is a growing movement in the community to start up a theater."

Erik caught the expression of confusion cross his wife's face, but he could see the situation clearly now. "You've heard right," he answered. "And the rest of what you've probably heard is correct as well. Clarette here is the driving force behind it. In fact, the project was her idea in the first place."

"As a new Christian," Exa Belle said, directing her dark gaze toward Clarette, "you of course could not be expected to know this, but the theater, as well as the moving pictures, is a source of ungodly entertainment. As a church body, we disdain such things."

"Not only do we refrain from attending," Wilma put in quickly, "but we would never be involved in any part of the promotion of such evil things."

"Where you come from," Marion picked up the refrain, "I'm sure the theater was part of your lifestyle. But now that you're here, now that you're walking the narrow road, things should be..."

Clarette's face had gone pale. She set her cup aside on the nearby desk. "Why don't all of you stop dancing around the subject and get to the point," she blurted out. "Whatever you've come here to say, just say it!"

Exa Belle looked at Reverend Dabney waiting. The man's eyes were empty. Erik wondered what it must be like to be controlled by a woman like Widow Traeger?

"That's all right, Reverend," Erik spoke up. "You don't have to say a thing. I believe the message has come through pretty clear. You're here to deliver the ultimatum. Either Clarette ceases her work with the theater, or she'll be asked to leave the church. How close am I?"

Reverend Dabney shook his head. "It's not because we don't like your wife, Erik," he said as though Clarette were not sitting right there. "But we have a testimony to uphold in the community. We must uphold our beliefs in whatever way we can."

"Even if it means kicking someone out of the church?" Erik demanded.

"Oh, we'd never do that," Marion gushed. "We're not kicking anyone out." She looked at Clarette. "Really, Mrs. Torsten, Exa Belle has been very kind about this. She said that once you knew the truth of the situation, you'd want to do what's right. For the sake of the church, for sake of your husband's integrity, and for your own soul."

Clarette was shaking her head. She shot Erik a wide-eyed look. "Erik, this isn't making any sense to me."

"To me either." Erik stood and walked to the bedroom. "I hate to cut this visit short," he said, dragging wet coats from where they'd been draped across the bed, "but I believe there's nothing more to be said here."

"Really, Mr. Torsten," Exa Belle said, as she took her coat and struggled into it with no assistance. "I was so sure you would be reasonable about this."

"I don't believe you thought that for a moment," Erik replied, his anger mounting. "I believe you've been looking for months for a way to remove Clarette from the midst of your church."

"I've never thought such a thing in my life. And why do you say *my* church? Why it's certainly not my church."

"It's not?" He jabbed a thumb toward the pastor. "Well, it's certainly not his. And I wonder if it's even God's."

"If that's the way you feel," Exa Belle huffed, "there are plenty other more *liberal* churches in town that might be more to your liking."

They were at the door now, grabbing umbrellas. Erik held the door wide open. "You may be right, Widow Traeger. Good night."

The rain was still drumming down noisily, dripping off the eaves of the front porch in sheets. There was nothing more to be said as the grim entourage made their way through deep puddles to the waiting touring car. Reverend Dabney looked thinner than ever draped in his large raincoat. Dutifully, he opened car doors for the ladies and assisted with their umbrellas before going around to the driver's side and getting in.

As they drove off, Erik closed the door and turned and pulled Clarette to him and held her tight. He couldn't believe what he'd just heard. How dare they lash out at his wife? How dare they?

"Are they right, Erik?" she asked, her voice small. "Am I going against God?"

"It doesn't matter, Clarette. You have to answer to your own conscience. You can't allow them to be your conscience."

"I didn't mean to embarrass you. I want to be a good wife, Erik. I never thought my ideas would bring such humiliation down on you. I'm so sorry."

Erik cupped her face in his hands and looked into her eyes. Eyes that were usually bright with hope and excitement, now troubled and rimmed in tears. "Listen to me, Mrs. Torsten. You have never, never been an embarrassment to me. I've never been so proud of you as my wife." He pulled his handkerchief from his pocket and touched at her tears. "I'm the one who should be apologizing to you. I'm the one who subjected you to this."

Kissing her gently, he said, "Come on now. I'll help you with the dishes, then let's get some sleep."

Long after Clarette had fallen asleep, he tossed fitfully trying to get those harsh judgmental faces from his mind. He wanted to hate them for hurting Clarette, and yet he knew he needed to forgive.

What's going on, Lord? Everything seems to be going so sour. What am I supposed to do?

It didn't seem he'd slept at all, and yet the pounding on the back door shocked him from a deep sleep. Before he could grab his robe, shouting sounded along with the pounding.

"Torsten! Get dressed. Water's rising!"

Erik hit the light switch, but the electricity was gone. He opened the back door off the kitchen to see Graham Cooper who owned the hardware store. Past him through the rain, he saw other men with flashlights running from house to house. Erik had lived by the Caney River for years and had witnessed this scene countless times. But Clarette had not. The men usually sent the women and children to higher ground while they fought the water in town.

He chided himself now. He'd been so angry about the visit from the church, he'd let himself become lax. He should have been up watching with the others.

"What is it?" Clarette asked.

"The Caney's flooding," he said pulling on trousers and a wool shirt. "Get dressed. Trousers preferably and your boots. Grab a few things and put in the car." He pulled his old felt hat from the top of the closet.

"What'll I take? Where'll I go?" He could hear panic rising in her voice. "What are you going to do?"

He stopped a moment and took her by the shoulders. "Don't be afraid, Clarette. All you need to do is drive up to Dewey. We'll get Dovey, and any other women from the neighborhood who'll go with you. The hotel up there will let you stay. Or perhaps they'll have a building at the fairgrounds open. The people around here are used to this."

"But what about you?"

"I'll be helping with sandbagging." He'd released her now and she was pulling on her boots and coat.

"I could help do that," she told him. "I want to stay with you."

"I have no doubt you could, my darling. But Dovey needs you."

"Why can't we just stay in the house? You told me once this was the high end of town."

"It is, but no sense taking a chance getting stranded. I'll pull the car up to the door."

As he suspected, she loaded the typewriter, her script, and the silver set, which they'd still not had time to sell. The lady living on the other side of Dovey, named Martha—also a widow—agreed to ride along.

Dovey had been up all night and much of her valuables had been taken to the attic. When Erik saw it, he again mentally kicked himself. He should have been doing the same thing. As he helped Dovey to the car, she was in her usual jovial joking mood. She'd be good for Clarette.

When everything was ready, he and Clarette paused for a moment on the back porch holding one another. "You'll be all right?" she questioned.

He kissed her wet face. "I'll be fine, and so will you."

"Erik? What about the office?"

He steered her gently out into the pouring rain and opened the car door. "I can't tell you, Clarette. I just don't know."

He helped her in and closed the door.

She cranked the window down just a bit. "I love you, Erik."

"I love you, too. I'll try to call you later in the afternoon. That is, if the phones aren't all out."

As he watched the headlights of the Model T poking holes through the dark rain, he wondered if perhaps it wouldn't be a blessing if the Caney washed the *Courier* all the way down to Catoosa.

Chapter 10

The highway from Bartlesville to Dewey was a soupy mess. However, there were other cars traveling the same way and Clarette had no fear. If she had been afraid, Dovey's lively spirit would have chased it away. Dovey told flood stories from years gone by, and then decided it would be fitting to sing the old hymn, "Higher Ground." The very idea of it had the three of them laughing gaily as they puttered along.

In the town of Dewey, veterans of past floods had already arrived. Dovey explained that some had probably arrived the evening before, especially mothers with small children. Since the hotel was filled—even the downstairs parlor was crammed with people—Dovey instructed Clarette to drive to the fairgrounds. The town of Dewey was a good deal smaller than Bartlesville, and within minutes they were parked in front of a long low brick exhibit building. Once inside they were welcomed by a group of Dewey's church women who distributed blankets, sandwiches, and tin cups of coffee. Among the dozens of others, they settled in to wait out the remainder of the night.

Clarette was a muddle of confusion as the memory of the previous evening clouded her mind. Several times, she considered broaching the subject with Dovey, but then thought better of it. After all, it wasn't Dovey's problem, and what could she do about it anyway? The question she most wanted to ask was whether or not Exa Belle and the others were right about the theater being evil. But she was also afraid of the answer. If Dovey agreed, it would be more than Clarette could stomach just now.

The hours dragged out as daylight came and morning melted into afternoon. Clarette felt her head would burst from the din of noise echoing in the building. Periodically, she stepped outside and stood under the wide eaves. The rain was letting up. She hoped they wouldn't have to spend the night here. She tried to pray, but the worry about Erik kept overpowering the prayers.

At one point when she was studying the gray skies, Dovey appeared beside her. "For a Yankee, and a New Yorker at that, you sure been quiet today. Something on your mind?"

Dear sweet Dovey. "Something is on my mind. A rather complicated something."

"We got time. Don't look like we're going anywhere just yet."

Clarette thought a moment. Perhaps there was a way to ask without really asking. "Tell me, Dovey. The Bible doesn't actually give us answers for everything does it? I mean, it can't cover everything."

Dovey gave a grin that showed her pink gums. She had a few teeth left in her head, but not many. "You reckon you couild get to the point?"

"Well, there are things in the world today that couldn't possibly be mentioned in the Bible. How's a person supposed to know if something is right or wrong?"

"The Bible is like a map, honey. Like a guide book. Like a measuring stick. It don't have to name every little thing. You get close enough to Jesus, there's just some things you don't want to do no more. He sorta purifies your desires."

Clarette knew that for a fact; it had happened to her. But that didn't help with this mess about the theater. "What if someone says something is wrong and you don't think is wrong?"

"Our smart God gave each one of us a conscience. When you belong to the Lord, and when you stay close to Him, you'll feel that conscience prick."

"That seems so arbitrary. I wish I had a more definite gauge to go by."

Dovey shrugged. "It's been working since Adam and Eve. Why do you think Adam hid from God after they tasted the forbidden fruit?" She waggled a thin wrinkled finger. "His conscience was hurtin' him somethin' awful. If it worked for Adam, it'll work for you." That said, she turned and went back inside leaving Clarette to continue to sort out the confusion.

That evening word came that the waters were receding, and that the Caney had not crested as high as had been predicted. With great relief, Clarette, Dovey, and Martha piled in the Model T for the drive home. The water had come within a few blocks of their neighborhood, but all was safe and dry.

The report of downtown wasn't as good, they were told. Nearly every building had been flooded. Clarette knew that meant the *Courier* as well. She hadn't expected Erik to be at the house and she was right. However, to her delight, his voice came on the line when she called the office, so the phone lines were intact. He was there scooping out smelly silt and mud he told her. He was thankful she was home and that she'd made the trip all right.

"I want to come down and help," she told him. She hadn't slept at all the night before, but she didn't feel tired. She wanted to be with him. "Can I drive through downtown?"

"There's no sense in you being in this mess."

"Your old galoshes are out on the porch," she said. "I'll put them on and be there as soon as I can. I'll bring sandwiches."

He still protested, but she interrupted, telling him she loved him and that she'd see him shortly. Quickly she put together a few sandwiches and filled the Thermos with coffee, and pulling on his galoshes, she was on her way. Parking nearly a block away, she waded through the muck to the office.

The pale glow of lanterns lit many of the stores where men were working with shovels and push-brooms to clean up the mess. Thankfully, the night was clear with a bright moon. As soon as Erik saw her coming, he threw down his shovel and ran to grab her almost making her drop the things she was carrying.

"How bad is it?" she asked as he led her inside. But he didn't have to answer. Her heart sank when she saw the mess. They worked side by side without talking through the night, stopping only to grab a bite to eat. She was glad she'd come to help. At various intervals, other people, some they knew—some they didn't, came in to lend a hand. It seemed the whole town had turned out to help in the cleanup efforts. Clarette was grateful, but she didn't see how they would ever recover from this disaster.

With the dawn came brilliant sunshine, the heat of which caused the odors of stagnant water and fishy river silt to grow to overpowering intensity.

At about ten in the morning, when Clarette thought surely she would faint from the smell or collapse from exhaustion, Erik said, "Let's stop a while and go get breakfast." Together they walked to a restaurant at the far end of town, which had been out of reach of the waters. One of the only eating places spared, it was crowded with people.

As they were eating breakfast, George Cox, owner of the *Magnet* came in, saw them sitting there and came to their table. "Mornin' Erik, Clarette. I been by your place just now."

Clarette looked up at the tall rugged-looking man. Why would he be concerned about them when his own building was probably hit worse than theirs?

"Muddy mess just like all the rest of town," Erik quipped. His tone was noncommittal. Although George represented the competition, she knew Erik respected him.

"May I sit down?" he asked.

"Sure," Erik answered, pulling out an empty chair.

George removed his Stetson, hung it on the nearby rack and sat down. Waving the waitress over, he ordered steak and eggs and coffee.

As he ate he talked generally about the flood, but once he had swiped up the last bit of egg yolk with his biscuit, he looked at Erik and said, "Torsten, tell you what. I'd like to buy you out lock, stock, and barrel. Equipment, subscribers everything. I don't want to insult you, but I know the flood could be a crowning blow to you."

Erik sat there for a moment. When he started to speak George held up his hands to stop him. Scooting back his chair he said, "Don't answer me yet. The two of you need to talk about it." He grabbed the Stetson, placed it on his head and tapped the crown. "If you're interested then I'll make an offer and we can go from there." And he walked out.

Clarette dared not say a word, but waited for Erik to comment, but he said nothing. Through the rest of the day they cleaned and worked as much as they could. When their place was relatively clear of mud, they went down the street to see where they could be of assistance elsewhere. It was nearly midnight when they collapsed into bed.

It wasn't until they were at the breakfast table the next morning that Erik finally said to her, "What do you think of George's offer?"

"I don't know what to think. I'm still in shock."

"I've been doing a lot of soul searching, Clarette. I think this is an answer to prayer."

She nodded. "Maybe so." She'd not experienced enough answered prayers to be sure.

"We can at least listen to his offer."

"We can."

Erik reached for her hand. "And then what? What if we do sell out?"

"Let's get away for a while. We've been struggling for so many months. We need time to think."

"Get away, where?"

"New York."

"New York?"

She ignored the shock in his voice. Actually it was a new thought to her as well. It had only come to her after George made the offer. "You've never met my family. And while I admit they've cause me grief in the past, I would like to see them again, especially Grandmother Vanderpool. I'd love to show you around, and maybe..."

"Maybe what?"

"Maybe I could even take my play script around to a few places to see what kind of reaction I get."

He nodded and pursed his lips. He released her hand then and patted it gently. "It's something to consider," he said.

Clarette took heart. It wasn't a firm no, which she'd almost expected. "I could take you to see inside workings of a really big newspaper and introduce you to the editor." Seeing the interest flickering in his eyes, she went on telling him other sights in and around New York that she'd love for him to see. "And the time away can give us time to think and pray about what to do next."

"Clarette, is this partly because what happened with Exa Belle Traeger? Is that why you want to leave?"

"I don't know." She struggled to be as honest as she could. "I guess that could be part of it. But if it is, is that wrong?"

Erik rose and pulled her to her feet and held her close. "No darling. That's not wrong. Do you want to go with me to talk to George?"

She shook her head. "I'm terrible at negotiations. You go."

Kissing her warmly, he said, "I love you, Clarette. Everything's going to be all right."

When he said it like that, she was sure it would be.

———⊙———

GEORGE'S OFFER WAS more than generous and fair. Two busy weeks were spent closing out accounts, meeting with accountants and moving equipment out of the little *Courier* office. Then they stored what little household furniture they had with Erik's parents and cleared out of the rental house. Clarette even met with the backers of the proposed little theater and helped them to find another person to head up the drive.

Erik placed a long-distance call to Tulsa to let Gaven and Tessa know they'd be gone for a while. Clarette listened as the two war buddies bantered back and forth. She could tell from Erik's remarks that Gaven was teasing him about not being able to find his way around the big city. After a few moments, Erik motioned for her to come closer, and held the receiver so both could listen at once.

"When you get tired of all that big city stuff," Gaven was saying, "come on back to Tulsa. Things are quiet here now."

"Now that we're not there," Erik quipped making Clarette chuckle.

"Hey, buddy. Tessa and I raised a ruckus or two ourselves remember?"

"I remember."

"Oh," Gaven added, "and be sure to tell Clarette that the Tulsa Little Theater is up and running."

"I'm right here listening, Gaven," she said. Erik corresponded with Gaven often, and he'd informed him about her work in starting up the theater project. She wasn't sure if Erik had told him about the pastor's visit.

"No legwork required here, Clarette," Gaven went on. "The theater is in full operation. They'd probably love to see your play."

Clarette looked up at Erik but was unable to read his reaction. To Gaven, Erik said, "And I suppose you think I should come back under the thumb of a man like Abram Schoggen."

Gaven's tone softened then. "I'm not trying to plan your life, buddy, but there's a whole lot more in Tulsa besides the newspapers."

"Thanks Gaven," Erik said. "I appreciate your concern, but we've not decided anything just yet. For now, we're going to take the money from the sale of the *Courier* and relax for a few days."

"Keep close watch on him, Clarette," Gaven said laughing. "When we were in New York after coming back from Europe, he nearly went nuts. Never did know where he was."

"Don't believe him," Erik said to Clarette. Then to Gaven, "And you stop giving her bad ideas."

Now they were back to their usual bantering-selves. Clarette gave a quick good-bye to both Gaven and Tessa and went back to her packing. But she kept thinking about Gaven's invitation for them to return to Tulsa. Maybe...

Saying good-bye to Dovey was difficult. "I know you may be back," Dovey said, "but you won't be my neighbors then."

Clarette thanked her repeatedly for all her help and together they wept at parting. That was the only sad moment for Clarette, because suddenly they were free from the tremendous pressure which had plagued them for months. When they boarded the train bound for the East Coast, they acted as silly and lighthearted as two school children. The three-day trip was a delight, and Clarette was falling in love with her husband all over again.

"We'll get the most difficult part over with first," she assured him the evening before they were to arrive in New York City.

"Meeting your family?"

She nodded. She'd wired ahead to let them know they were coming, and she knew this wouldn't be easy for Erik. "We'll just stay there a couple of days. Most of the time we'll be sightseeing in the city."

"I'm following you," he said.

"But you'll love Grandmother Vanderpool. She's not like the rest. And I know she'll love you too. You'll see."

———————◉———————

SEEING NEW YORK AGAIN brought a flood of memories to Erik's mind. Upon his return from France, he and his buddies had scoured the place seeing as many sights as possible before departing their separate ways for home. To think the long war was actually over had been like walking in a dream-world. Dressed in their smart uniforms, the soldiers received praise and smiles and encouragement wherever they went. A few restaurants even treated them to free meals.

Erik remembered how crowded and stifling the big city felt to him then, but with Clarette by his side it would be different. This was her home and he was confident this place would help him to know her better, and he was up for the challenge. After all, she'd put up with Bartlesville for all these months, a few weeks in the Big Apple couldn't be that bad.

It was early morning when they disembarked at noisy, crowded Pennsylvania Station. As they pushed through the crowds, strange food smells from assorted vendors assaulted Erik's nose.

Clarette was vibrant, her eyes alive with excitement. "Isn't it wonderful?" she said, gazing about. Her heels clicked merrily on the marble floor as she directed him through the mammoth station. After they'd gathered their baggage, she pointed out to him on the wall charts which train they would take across the Hudson River to Hamptonwood, New Jersey to the Vanderpool estate.

With tickets in hand, she said, "We have a few minutes. Let's go find a hot dog vendor. I'm starving for a good New York hot dog."

To Erik the New York hot dog tasted no different than the ones he used to buy at the Coney Islander eatery in Tulsa, but Clarette insisted the flavor was altogether different.

Within the hour they were back aboard another train on their way to the Jersey side of the river.

She had instructed her family not to meet them, for they didn't know what time they would arrive. Since mid-day at the Hamptonwood station was fairly quiet, they easily found a taxi.

Clarette's light-hearted chatter along the way described her growing up years in the rambling old stone house outside Hamptonwood, including the fun and games she and Aubert enjoyed together. "That was before the money and success spoiled him," she added. Later, she pointed out the road that led to that special old house.

That meant they were only two miles from their destination. Taking hold of Erik's arm and snuggling close to him in the back seat of the roomy cab, she said, "Now let me warn you again, don't let anything overwhelm you." She'd repeated the remark a number of times during their train ride to New York. "Promise me?" she added.

"I promise."

But when they turned into the shady wooded drive leading to the estate, he began to wonder if he could keep that promise. Gazing out the window he took in the sprawling buff-stucco edifice with red tiled roof and let out a low whistle. It looked like it belonged on a bluff overlooking the Mediterranean

No oil man in Oklahoma had created anything like this storybook place.

Chapter 11

The cabbie drove past the three-tiered fountain right up to the broad expanse of black marble entry stairs which led to the magnificent home.

"Whatta joint!" the fellow exclaimed around a wad of chewing gum. "Do you gotta get engraved invitations to come here?" He hopped out to assist with the bags.

Erik and Clarette came around to the back of the car. Erik grabbed one of the bags and Clarette took her small train case. "No invitations," Erik quipped, leaning toward the cabbie and lowering his voice. "But it helps to be on speaking terms with your in-laws."

Struggling with the load of luggage, the cabbie abruptly stopped and stared at him. "You ain't fooling me? Your in-laws? Honest?"

"Do I look like an honest fellow?"

By now Clarette was giggling.

"You sure do," the cabbie answered.

Erik took Clarette's arm as they went up the series of steps. "At least I think they're on speaking terms with me."

"Well, of course they are, silly," Clarette answered. "Why wouldn't they be?"

"Oh sure. You're right. Why wouldn't they be? Could it be because they just haven't met me yet?"

Clarette poked him in the ribs. "Now stop that."

But he had to say something to fight down the nervousness that had suddenly attacked him. He'd not been cotton-mouth since he's come home from the war. The embarrassment frustrated him.

"This is as far as I go," the cabbie said, huffing to catch his breath at the top of the stairs.

Erik reached for his wallet and paid the man while Clarette rang the bell. Watching the cab drive away, Erik felt somewhat stranded. Just as he expected, a prim straight-backed butler answered the door.

"Just like the movies," he whispered.

"Wait'll you meet the cast," she whispered back, grinning.

"Good day, Miss Clarette. Your father's in the library. He's expecting you."

"He stayed home from the office?"

"Yes ma'am he did."

Erik looked at her surprised expression, and wondered what father *wouldn't* stay home for a daughter who'd been away for almost a year.

"We'd like to freshen up first," Clarette told the butler, whose name was Gibbons.

"Of course." He picked up luggage, but didn't huff up the stairs as the cabbie had.

Erik tried his best not to rubberneck as they followed Gibbons up the carpeted stairs, around the ornately carved balustrade, and down a long hallway.

"Where's mother?" Clarette asked as Gibbons opened the door to a large room all decked out in feminine pastel colors.

Gibbons set down the luggage then stood straight. Erik wondered if he had a board in his shirt. "Mrs. Vanderpool is in the garden. Shall I tell her you're here?"

"Please."

"Very well ma'am. Anything else?"

Clarette shook her head. "Nothing, thank you."

When the door had closed, and Gibbons gone, Erik said, "What do you mean *'nothing.'* We could have ordered room service for supper."

She laughed and grabbed him around the waist. "That would be fun. Why didn't I think of it?"

Erik surveyed the room, taking in the large canopied bed with cherry wood steps at the side. Heavy ornate pieces of dark furniture were strategically set about, making the rosebud wallpaper seem soft and dainty in contrast. Through the door to the adjoining bathroom he saw that the marble sink was fitted with gold spigots. One of those crazy spigots would have probably paid to save the *Courier*.

"I take it this was your room?" he said with a wave of his hand.

"Actually, I'd left home by the time they built this place, but this room was designated as mine. Mother continued hoping I'd straighten up and come back here to live." She gave Erik a squeeze. "But I didn't."

He looked down at her expressive dark eyes. "Didn't straighten up, or didn't come back?" he teased.

"According to my parents, neither one! Come on now," she said pulling away. "Let's get ready to go down and meet Mother and Father."

Once again, Erik's palms became clammy.

In a few minutes, Clarette was leading him by the hand through a tricky maze of hallways and down back staircases to the library.

The meeting with the Vanderpools was more uncomfortable than Erik could ever have imagined. Didn't these people ever laugh or have fun? They didn't appear particularly overjoyed to see their daughter. He watched as Clarette went to her father, kissing him lightly and giving a little hug.

Mr. Vanderpool's tailored suit, stiff collar, and bright gold watch fob spoke volumes to Erik. The man probably dressed that way every day of his life. He held his pince-nez glasses in his hand until Clarette made the polite introduction, then he secured them firmly on his nose as though to study Erik thoroughly. Erik stepped over to shake hands with his father-in-law, still self-conscious about his sweaty palms. The man remained seated in the wing-back chair.

"It's good that we're finally able to meet you," Mr. Vanderpool said simply.

Clarette was pulling Erik's hand guiding him to where her mother sat in a matching wing-back chair closer to the massive stone fireplace. Another light kiss, another little hug resulting in very little response.

Viletta Fortier Vanderpool was a strikingly beautiful woman. Same dark eyes and hair as Clarette's. Same flawless olive complexion.

"Mrs. Vanderpool," he said, after Clarette had introduced him, "now that I've met you, I know where my wife inherited her beauty."

The dark eyes failed to respond. "Flattery costs little, Mr. Torsten. We're very pleased you've decided to bring Clarette home for a visit. Please make yourself at home while you're a guest here. We'd like you to stay as long as you please, since it's so seldom we get to see our daughter."

The words made Erik feel as though he'd kidnapped Clarette right from her bedroom. He found himself wondering if these parents had any inkling of what a jewel they had in Clarette.

Following the stiff introductions, a polite and formal conversation ensued. A few questions were directed at Erik, mostly concerning what he was doing, and what he planned to do in the future. A couple of times, Clarette jumped in and answered, explaining that they were both taking time away to think. The response to that remark was a low-throated "Hmm," from Mrs. Vanderpool. Mr. Vanderpool removed his pince-nez, gazed at Erik, then returned them to his nose.

They were served tea in cups so tiny, Erik wasn't sure he could keep hold of the handle. When he'd finished with the tea, and the small light cookies, he felt he hadn't eaten at all and was ready to go searching for the kitchen pantry.

Just when he didn't think he could stand another moment of the stuffiness, Clarette stood to her feet. "It's been a long trip. I think we'll relax in the garden until dinner."

"Yes, go along," Mrs. Vanderpool said as though talking to two ten-year-olds. "Aubert and his wife and your grandmother will be here for dinner."

"Oh good!"

Erik saw Clarette brighten. He remembered all the good things she'd told him about Grandmother Vanderpool.

"You've not met Divone," Mrs. Vanderpool continued, referring to Aubert's bride. "An absolutely lovely girl. And their wedding was lovely as well."

"I'm sure it was lovely, Mother," Clarette answered as she inched them toward the door. "We'll see you at dinner."

Erik opened the library door and they escaped.

Strolling with Clarette through winding paths of formal gardens that sunny afternoon was almost heavenly. Precisely-trimmed privet hedges bordered flower beds filled with banks of blossoms, reminiscent of one of his mother's colorful quilts. Here and there they came upon a sparkling fountain, or quiet fish pond, where they sat and relaxed in serene peace.

The large blue-tiled swimming pool and surrounding bathhouses made Erik wish it were warm enough for a dip. Instead they took off their shoes and let their feet dangle in the shallow end, talking and enjoying the perfect day and one another.

"I think," he told her as they sat by the swimming pool, "that I've been duly repaid."

"Repaid?"

"Yes. Repaid for every uncomfortable, awkward moment you ever spent in Bartlesville, Oklahoma."

Her clear laugh rang out. "They are two very different places, aren't they? And here we are stuck in the middle."

He put his arm around her shoulders and pulled her close. "Stuck in the middle, perhaps. But very much stuck on each other." He tipped up her face and enjoyed a warm, lingering kiss.

DINNER WAS A TIME OF mixed emotions. Erik was told by Clarette to wear his best suit, which he'd purchased on sale in Zofness Brothers' bargain basement in Bartlesville. It would have to do, but he fought all evening with the feeling of appearing horribly backwoodsy.

When he walked into the formal dining room and saw the long table set with silver and crystal and pure white linen, beneath massive glittering chandeliers, the feeling intensified.

Grandmother Vanderpool was the saving grace of the evening. Just as Clarette had described, she was lively, sharp, and full of good humor. Erik couldn't help but feel that her twinkling eyes were laughing at the roomful of stuffy people surrounding her.

When Clarette first introduced Erik to her grandmother, the stout, gray-haired lady shook his hand with a firm grip.

"Clarette tells me you're a Christian, and that you were instrumental in Clarette giving her life to the Lord. For that, you're tops in my book."

Instinctively, Erik put his arm about her shoulder and whispered his thanks for her vote of confidence in him.

At dinner, several servants whisked in and out of the room deftly serving each course. Clarette had already briefed him on how to choose which piece of silverware and when. He was situated directly across from Clarette's brother, Aubert who was a replica of his father with the same straight long nose, same masked expression. Only his dark slicked-back hair and slender build were different.

Clarette seemed more at ease with her grandmother by her side. In answers to her questions, Clarette told some about Oklahoma and the work they'd done on the *Courier*.

"We had the last say in our paper," she said to her father. "No one told us what stories we could or couldn't print."

"Yes," came the answer, "and you saw how long it lasted. If you're not connected to the AP these days, no one cares a hoot about what you have to say."

Erik knew he was speaking truth, but he also knew the remark and the tone hurt Clarette deeply.

Aubert's wife appeared to have been hand-picked for him. Her poise, control and manners echoed those about her. At one point she asked, "Tell me, what is the Wild West really like?"

To which Erik glibly answered, "It was pretty good until all the Easterners came in tearing up the countryside digging for oil."

The subject changed after that and no one asked him any more questions.

Following supper, Erik was invited to the smoking room with the men. He gave Clarette a look and slight nod as though he were doomed to muddle through it.

Erik followed the father and son downstairs into a darkly paneled room where a billiard table had been set up in the middle of the room. Overstuffed butternut-colored chairs clustered about a low, thick-legged, leather-covered table. Large murals and prints of clipper ships were hung in every spare bit of wall space. Deep bay windows were adorned in heavy maroon drapes from ceiling to floor.

Erik politely refused a cigar from the proffered humidor. Though not a connoisseur of cigars, he recognized them as Havana's best. On the heels of that, he refused the cocktail that Aubert had so expertly mixed. The refusal seemed to be agreeable with Aubert who quickly downed them both.

As they sat about in the smoke-filled room, Mr. Vanderpool gave Erik a history lesson of the Vanderpool Silk Company which began with his grandfather. He told of the courageous journeys that his father and his grandfather made to the Orient aboard clipper ships, not only to trade for silk, but also to learn all they could about the exotic fabric.

"Since then," he said, blowing a stream of smoke into the air, "our only diversification has been the garment industry."

"And stocks," Aubert put in.

"I was speaking of business, not investments," Mr. Vanderpool contradicted him quickly. "Our garment factories down on Fifth Street are some of the finest in Manhattan. We treat employees fairly, and turn out high quality products."

Erik wasn't sure how to answer except for nods and "Hmm hmn's." He knew absolutely nothing about textiles, fabrics, or clothing manufacturing. Frankly, he found the subject frightfully boring.

"Our stocks steadily increase from year to year, and our board of directors consists of men of high standing in the city. In our field of endeavor, we are without parallel." He sipped the cocktail in his hand while Aubert mixed himself a third. Erik shifted in the soft leather chair, wishing there were some way of escape.

After the extended dissertation, Mr. Vanderpool finally came to the point. He replaced his pince-nez and leaned forward in his chair. "Now that you are unemployed, Mr. Torsten, and since you are now a member of this family, I'm pleased to be able to offer you a managerial position in my factory which manufactures fine silk shirts for men."

Erik started to speak and tell this man he was not interested in such a position, but Mr. Vanderpool raised his hand to silence him.

Aubert who'd been tapping a few billiards into the pockets spun around. "Father! Managerial?"

"Hush, Aubert."

Aubert hushed.

"Now then," Mr. Vanderpool continued. "I realize you would need training, but I have key people who've been in the industry for years and can teach you the ropes quickly." He leaned back as though it were all settled. "I have no doubt you're a hard worker. Probably came from very good stock."

Erik felt like a steer on his way to the slaughter house.

"No offense, Mr. Torsten." Mr. Vanderpool waved his hand in a broad sweep. "But the newspaper business is dead end. It's going nowhere. I strongly advise you to get out and stay out."

Finally, there came a silence and Erik realized he was now expected to respond. He cleared his throat. No one had offered him even a glass of water or a sarsaparilla and the smoke was beginning to burn. He scooted forward in his chair in order to make a quick exit when he could. "Thank you very much, sir, for your generous offer." He hoped that sounded sincere. "I know you not only have my good in mind, but the good of your daughter."

He chose this moment to stand. "But I have no interest at all in burying myself in the garment industry of New York City. While I may not be sure what I'm going to do at this moment, I'm quite sure of what I don't want to do. Now if you'll excuse me, it's been a long day."

At the door he stopped and turned. Mr. Vanderpool's face had gone pale. "Oh, and if I do agree that the newspaper business is a dead end, I'll make the decision myself whether or not to stay out."

And he was out the door and free. Now if he could just find his way back to their bedroom.

Chapter 12

Clarette nervously paced the floor of the pink bedroom. What could be taking Erik so long? What was her father up to? She simply couldn't trust him. She hoped against hope that he wasn't castigating Erik, or humiliating him in any way. If he did, she knew she'd never want to come back here ever again.

When the door finally opened, she flew to him. "Are you all right?"

Wrapping his arms around her, he chuckled softly. "I feel like a rat in a maze. You should have told me to leave a trail of bread crumbs so I could find my way back."

"I should have come to get you."

"Why didn't you? I would have appreciated a rescue."

"I got to talking with Grandmother Vanderpool and forgot the time. I just now came up. Come out here," she said, taking him by the hand. "Let's sit out on the balcony and you can tell me all about it."

"I need a glass of water first," he said.

"I have lemonade out here. Room service, remember?"

They settled into the wicker furniture and sipped lemonade in the cool air of the spring evening.

After he relayed the long conversation to Clarette, she just shook her head. "I never in a million years dreamed he'd offer you a job. He was doing that for me. He thinks I need rescuing."

"I figured that."

When he told his response to the offer she had to laugh. "I'm proud of you, Erik. It's nice for Father to learn that some people can't be bought." She leaned her head back into the soft cushions. "I can tell you one thing—Grandmother Vanderpool thinks you're wonderful."

"One strike and three outs," he quipped. "Four, counting Aubert's wife."

"I'm sorry it's been so difficult."

"As difficult as a committee from church?" he asked, and they laughed together at the shared joke. "What exactly did Grandmother Vanderpool say about me?" he wanted to know.

"She commended me that I'd made an excellent choice of a husband. And I told her she didn't even know the half."

Erik smiled and Clarette could sense he was relaxing from the grueling ordeal. "We'll continue to stay here a few days," she told him, "but we'll stay so busy we won't have time for all the folderol here."

"Sounds good to me."

"Come on. Let's get some sleep."

As they were getting ready for bed, Erik called out to her from the bathroom. "Hey, tell me something. If I did take your father up on his offer, would that mean I'd get free silk shirts? That might be tempting."

She threw a soft fluffy pink slipper at him, but she missed.

———●———

THE NEXT MORNING EARLY, Clarette asked to borrow the Auburn coupe to drive to the station. Her mother offered her chauffeur and the touring car, but Clarette firmly turned her down.

"Just transportation to get us to the train station. Then we won't have to bother anyone if we come back late. We may take in a show this evening." She winked at Erik behind her mother's back so he'd know she was plotting to keep him out of that smoking room for the rest of their stay, if possible.

As they went out to the garage, Clarette could tell Erik was a bit nervous about driving the expensive automobile, so she offered to drive. When he readily agreed, she knew she'd done the right thing.

In Hamptonwood, she parked the Auburn and they boarded the limited to Manhattan. Later, when they stepped off the train at Pennsylvania Station, Erik asked, "Where first?"

Walking from the bustling station out into the warm sunshine, Clarette looked around soaking up the sights and gazing at the familiar surroundings. Since it was Saturday, the streets weren't quite as crowded as on weekdays. She took a deep breath. It was good to be back.

"Let's see," she said, pausing a moment to think. "I'd like to call my old roommate Herta and see if she's home today. If she is, we'll take the subway to Brooklyn and I'll show you where I used to live."

She took Erik's hand and headed for the nearest telephone booth. "We'll see if she even has a telephone. She hated them when I first had it installed. She may have had it taken out again."

Her old number was given to the operator, and soon she could hear it ringing on the other end, then Herta's strong voice came on with the hint of German accent. The stoic girl was seldom emotional, but Clarette could hear the excitement building in her voice. "You're here? Back here in New York?"

"Just for a visit," Clarette explained. "I wondered if you were up to having company. I'd like you to meet Erik, and I'd like him to see where I used to live."

"You come right ahead," she said in her matter-of-fact manner. "The coffee it will be ready by the time you arrive."

Clarette was nodding and smiling to Erik, who was leaning against the door of the booth. "Do you have a loaf of black bread made up?" Clarette asked.

"But of course. You miss it, eh?"

Clarette had to laugh. How she had disdained the dark heavy bread the first time she tasted it, but later she came to love it. "Hate to admit it, Herta, but you're right. We'll be there shortly."

Replacing the receiver, she said, "Let's go down to the subway. We're on our way to Flatbush!"

As the subway train rumbled along beneath the bustling city, Eric waved at the darkened window. "Great view. I like it."

She laughed at his humor. "You'll like Brooklyn," she assured him. "It has more of a small-town feel. And Coney Island is a splendid place to see the ocean and have a wonderful time."

He nodded and smiled making Clarette wish she could read his mind. She couldn't tell if he was impressed or not.

The walk from the end of the subway line to the place where Clarette used to live seemed to make Erik sit up take notice. The neighborhoods were laid out with tidy little yards, surrounded by picket fences, many with profusions of climbing roses draped over them. Backyards sported clean laundry hanging on the clotheslines flapping gently in the wind.

"You're right," he agreed. "This doesn't seem like New York at all. I kind of like this place."

Clarette gave a quiet sigh. Finally.

"This is it," she said as they approached a four-story brownstone.

"Mmm. Nice."

"Nothing fancy," she said. "But then I couldn't afford anything fancy."

"A far cry from the Vanderpool estate." He stopped and looked down at her for a moment. "I don't see how you did it."

"Did what?"

"Turned your back on the money and detached yourself from all the trappings."

She thought a moment. "It wasn't the trappings, Erik, it was being trapped. The attempts to stifle me made me feel like a caged animal. I had to break free."

He leaned down to kiss her forehead lightly. "My free-spirited little French girl."

"Come on. Let's go meet Herta."

Clarette was pleased at how relaxed Erik was with the German girl. He was a second-generation immigrant and they found they had much in common.

Herta hadn't changed much with her long dresses, dark stockings, and square-heeled shoes, but her laugh seemed to come more easily. As she sliced the dark bread and poured stout coffee, she didn't appear as different to Clarette as she used to. Even her dark hair pulled back in a severe bun, didn't look as old fashioned as it once did. In fact, Clarette thought it looked rather prim and tidy.

"Living room or kitchen?" Herta asked when the food was ready.

"Kitchen's fine with me," Erik replied.

"You have no roommate now?" Clarette asked as they scooted out the ladder-back chairs and sat down.

"One just left a week ago. The new one I found at the factory. She is to move in shortly."

"Oh good," Clarette said feeling relieved. She knew the rent here was too much for this girl's wages all alone.

When Erik offered to bless the food, Clarette smiled at her friend's look of surprise.

As they ate and chatted, Clarette was able to share with Herta her life-changing experience in Tulsa. How the fear of being kidnapped by the Klan had made her face her immortality.

"I was running headlong to find someone to tell me how to get to heaven."

Herta chuckled. "And here I could have told you long ago."

"You're so right, and I'm sorry I didn't listen. You and my Grandmother Vanderpool were both trying to tell me."

Erik reached out and put his arm about Clarette's shoulder. "Better late than never. Personally, I'm glad everything turned out just as it did." He paused. "Except for the whip on your back. I wouldn't wish that for anyone."

Clarette shuddered at the memory. "Don't remind me," she said. "But let's talk about lighter subjects."

"I would like to invite the two of you to visit our church service tomorrow morning," Herta put in. "That is, if you're looking for a place to worship."

Clarette hadn't even thought about it. It was so strange to think of attending church back here in New York. She looked at Erik.

"Don't look at me," he said with his hands up. "You're the one who's guiding this tour."

Smiling, Clarette said to Herta, "Thanks for the invitation. We might just take you up on it. We're trying to spend as little time at the castle as possible."

Herta nearly choked on her coffee at that remark. When she regained her composure, she chided her old friend. "You are to respect your family, Clarette, and honor your parents."

"You're right, Herta. But it's difficult at times."

Though the visit was a pleasant interlude in their day, there was much more to see and do.

"Where to next?" Herta asked as they prepared to leave.

"Back to Manhattan. I want to pay a visit to the *American*."

Herta gathered up the cups and plates and placed them beside the kitchen sink. "You suppose your old rival is still there?"

That remark piqued Erik's interest. "Rival?" he asked. "What rival?"

"You remember," Clarette said to Erik. "The reporter named Maxwell. I told you all about him. He didn't much like the thought of a woman usurping his territory."

"Funny," Erik said, smiling, "I love having you usurp my territory."

Herta laughed. "You got you a good fellow, Clarette. Even if you did have to go all the way to Oklahoma to find him."

Clarette grabbed Erik's hand. "God directed my steps."

"Right into my arms," Erik added.

"You are two lovebirds for certain." Herta followed them to the door. "I hope to see you tomorrow in church."

"You just might." Clarette gave a wave over her shoulder as they headed down the hall to the stairway. On the second floor, Clarette was surprised to see a sign that said, "Apartment for rent." These well-kept apartments were seldom empty. She said nothing, but tucked the information away for later.

On their way back downtown, Clarette explained to Erik about her former boss, Sid Epstein. "He's a tough editor. Nothing like Abram Schoggen." Mr. Schoggen had been Erik's boss in Tulsa—a soft, weak-kneed type of fellow, for whom Clarette had little respect.

Before going upstairs to the offices of the *American*, she guided Erik into a shop just inside the vast marble lobby. "Mr. Fabiano makes the best sausage in town, and we need a lunch break."

"I was hoping you had included lunch in our busy day," Erik teased.

At a table by the window they enjoyed a tasty lunch together while watching the crowded street outside.

"I bet this street is just as busy after dark," Erik said.

"You're right—especially after dark. Broadway is just a block over. The Great White Way. A very exciting place at night. You'll have to see it."

"With you, Clarette, everything's exciting."

She smiled as she savored his compliment. This trip was turning out to be the best thing that had ever happened to them. She felt like a bride all over again.

The newsroom of the *American* was the same noisy, smoke-filled din of hectic busyness. She didn't see Hank anywhere. Probably out on assignment.

Clarette walked up to the door which said "Editor," and rapped smartly, then heard a gruff, "Yeah. What do you want?" She pushed open the door. Seldom had she ever seen Sid Epstein off guard, but she definitely caught him off guard. The grizzled old editor nearly lost his stub of a cigar from his gaping mouth.

"Clarette Fortier, I never thought I'd see the likes of you back in New York ever again!" He jumped up from his creaking wooden chair and came to shake her hand. "Don't just stand there. Come in. Come in."

"Thanks, and it's Mrs. Torsten now."

Sid's craggy brows raised. "Is that right?" The short stocky man looked up at Erik who had thrust forth his hand.

"Erik Torsten's my name. Good to meet you. Clarette's told me you're a top-notch editor."

Returning his hand shake, Sid bit down on the cigar and said, "She said that? Even after I had to cut her off cold when she had a bundle of great stories."

"Oh Sid," Clarette gave a wave of her hand as she sat down in the chair he offered her. "I knew that wasn't your fault."

"Lotta things around here ain't my fault." After his guests were seated he plopped down in his chair again and pushed up to the desk. His rolled-up sleeves were soiled from all the papers he'd been working with that morning. He'd always refused to mess around with sleeve protectors.

"I never been no whiny baby, but the big boys take another little bite out of me each day." He rolled the cigar to the other side of his mouth and ran his fingers through his salt-and-pepper hair. "Mad dogs is what they are. But that's a whole other story. Tell me about Oklahoma."

"You don't have time to hear all about Oklahoma," she told him. "It's an absolutely fascinating place."

"You don't say. Sounded like a pretty dangerous place to me. Klan marches. Race riots. Don't sound too fascinating to this boy." He jabbed a stubby thumb at his chest.

"Oh, that's only a small part," Clarette protested.

"Tell him, Erik."

Erik gave a gentle shrug. "Since I grew up there, I'm afraid anything I said would be pretty biased."

"An honest guy, anyway," Sid stated. "I like that."

"We had our own newspaper in a town north of Tulsa called Bartlesville."

"You don't say." Sid leaned back and hooked his hands behind his head, the dead cigar stuck between two fingers. "What's this 'had' business?"

"We were flooded out a couple weeks ago," she explained.

"More of that fascinating place," Sid quipped with a slight grin.

She ignored the remark. "But we were struggling anyway."

"We found it pretty hard to be a weekly," Erik put in, "in a town with a large daily that had recently tapped into the AP."

Sid nodded. "Don't talk to this boy about competition. My life's overrun with competition." His tone of understanding took Clarette somewhat by surprise. What had she expected? She'd always known there was a kind, gentle man beneath the gruff exterior.

"So what now?" Sid asked.

Clarette kept quiet and let Erik answer. She wanted to hear how he expressed it.

"Now we're taking time off to think and plan," Erik said simply. "And sort out options."

Just then a knock came at the door. Sid rocked forward, slamming his hands on the desk. "Yeah. What do you want? Ain't you got no manners. I got company."

The door opened. A young blanched face appeared around the door. One who obviously hadn't yet seen past Sid's rough exterior. Clarette smiled inwardly. "Boss," he said in a soft voice. "I think we got a scoop on Izzy Eisenbaum."

Sid waved his hand impatiently. "Go chase after it. But you'll have a tough time getting there before the whole world."

The door slammed.

Erik glanced at Clarette then turned back to Sid. "We know Izzy."

"You don't say." The craggy brows were up again. "How would you two know a guy like that?"

Briefly Erik and Clarette explained how the well-known prohibition agent had come to the Glenn Pool to assist in breaking the bootlegging work of Hod Latham last winter. His work was instrumental in getting Gaven out of jail.

"That don't surprise me none. The guy is everywhere—all at once. He don't even look like no Fed man." He paused. "But I'm told that's why he shuts down more speakeasies and uncovers more illegal hootch than all them other so-called agents put together."

Clarette listened with interest. What a story that would make.

Later, as they rose to leave, Sid walked with them to the door and one more time expressed his pleasure at seeing Clarette again. He then surprised them both by addressing Erik. "Say, Mr. Torsten, I got need of another experienced reporter just now. Not easy to find someone who's been out there doin' it."

He waited, but Clarette and Erik just looked at him.

"Well, I mean youse is sorting out options." He punctuated his remark with a stab in the air with his cigar. "I just thought I'd give youse one more option to think about."

Chapter 13

Neither of them mentioned Sid's offer as they traveled about the city taking in the sights. But Clarette couldn't help but wonder what Erik thought.

Down at the Battery, they boarded the Staten Island Ferry, which cruised lazily out across the bay. Only a few high puffy clouds dotted the clear skies and the water was topped out with tiny white caps. Clarette insisted they sit on top so Erik could get the best view as they passed the tall, proud Statue of Liberty. Leaning on the railing, she pulled off her hat so she could feel the wind in her hair.

Later, on foot, they soaked up the distinct personalities of Chinatown and Little Italy. From there she took Erik up Broadway and pointed out the myriad of theaters in and around Times Square. In Bryant Park they relaxed on park benches beneath the shade trees and ate tasty hot roasted peanuts, feeding some to the pigeons as well.

It was while they were at Bryant Park that Clarette heard a familiar voice calling softly behind her. "Miss Clarie? That you, Miss Clarie?"

Whirling around, she saw her young friend, Spindle-Shanks. The shoe-shine boy was sitting sprawled out in the shade with his box beside him counting his coins.

"Shanks?" Jumping to her feet, Clarette walked across the grass to where the boy was now standing. "My gracious, you've grown a foot. I'm not sure I would have recognized you."

The ginger-colored boy gave a friendly grin. "You sure do look fine, Miss Clarie. I never thought I'd see you again. I wasn't even sure it was you. That's why I called out real quiet-like. I done heard you was out West somewheres."

"I was out West, but I'm back here on a visit. And there's someone I'd like you to meet." Turning back to where Erik waited she called him over.

"Erik," she said, "this young man is my friend, Spindle- Shanks, the person who has story tips galore. Shanks, this is my husband, Erik Torsten, from Oklahoma."

Sticking out a long arm, smiling more shyly now, Shanks grasped Erik's hand. "Pleased to meet you, sir. Welcome."

"Thank you, Shanks." Erik pointed to his shoes. "I sure could use a good shine."

Shank's black eyes brightened. "I gives the best."

Leading them back to the park bench, Shanks proceeded to whip up a shiny glow on Erik's tan calfskin shoes, dusty from all the walking they'd done.

With a couple of last snaps of his rag, Shanks stood to his feet. Clarette was amazed at how tall the youth had grown. "I'm on my way to Grand Central," he said, pocketing the coin Erik handed him. "'Bout time for the crowd to hit. Bye Miss Clarie. I mean, Mrs. Torsten. Right nice to see you again. Right nice." He waved his old slouch hat as he ran down East Forty-Second toward the station, the shoe-shine kit slapping against his side as he ran.

"That boy knows most every nook and cranny of this part of the city," she told Erik. "An amazing young man."

For supper, Clarette had great fun showing Erik the automat where they dropped nickels into slots and opened tiny doors to pull out their selections.

"They have the best corned beef in Manhattan," she told him.

With their trays filled, they poured tall glasses of milk from the golden fish-shaped spigots. They ate by the windows where they talked over the events of the day and watched as dusk gathered among the towering skyscrapers. In the back of her mind Clarette kept hearing Sid's job offer. She wondered if Erik had ignored it, or if he was quietly thinking about it. Either way, she was determined to leave it to him if he wanted to discuss it.

Each agreed they were much too tired for a show that evening—especially if they were to get up the next morning for church. "We'll go one evening next week," she suggested. "Then we'll have time to get all dressed up."

By seven that evening they were seated on a wooden bench in Pennsylvania Station waiting for their train to arrive. Erik's arm hung loosely on the back of the bench behind her.

"When we take in Broadway next week," she asked, looking up at him, "shall we see the Follies, or go to a play?"

"I have a wife who's writing a dramatic play and she asks if I want to go to the Follies? Perish the thought."

"You mean you'd really like to see a Broadway play?"

"I most certainly would."

"Erik," she said softly, laying her head on his shoulder. "You're too wonderful."

"Keep saying that and you'll have me believing it."

He started to lean down to kiss her, but the "all aboard" sounded for Hamptonwood causing them to jump to their feet and hurry toward the exit gate in order to get a good seat.

———◉———

CLARETTE WAS PLEASANTLY surprised at the friendliness of the old German church, which Herta and many of her family members attended. The large stone edifice was situated on a quiet corner near Brooklyn College, about ten blocks from Herta's apartment. Deep strong voices sang the sacred hymns with feeling, and the pastor seemed genuinely concerned for the souls of his flock.

Sitting among the congregation, many of whom still clung to old country ways in dress and speech, Clarette recalled the numerous times Herta had invited her to attend church before Clarette moved away.

How stubborn she'd been back then, not wanting to hear anything that had to do with Christianity. If only her heart had been open, these people no doubt would have loved her right into the Kingdom.

Following the service, Erik and Clarette politely turned down a number of invitations for Sunday dinner, not the least of which came from the pastor and his plump wife. But Clarette had already planned for her and Erik to have a picnic in Central Park.

"Perhaps if we're still here next Sunday," Erik tried to explain. "But our time is limited..."

"Ach," said Pastor Roswald with a wave of his hand, "Dinner does not take long, and you must eat somewhere."

They were difficult people to say no to. "Kindly persistent," Erik later described them.

Later as they strolled among the gardens of Central Park, they couldn't stop talking about not only the friendliness, but also the clear gospel message which had been presented at the little German church.

"What a refreshing change," Erik commented.

Clarette agreed, but was glad he was the one who said it and not her, knowing full well he was referring to the judgmental attitudes they'd recently encountered at First Church.

THE FOLLOWING WEDNESDAY evening they dressed to the teeth and even borrowed the Auburn coupe to drive to Manhattan for their night on the town. Clarette had nearly forgotten the breathtaking splendor of the Great White Way at night. Millions of dazzling, sparkling, blinking electric lights blazed before them as they motored down Broadway, making Clarette's pulse race crazily. What was it about this magic place that continued to excite her so?

The play they chose was superbly written and well directed. Clarette was more than a little impressed. All through the show, she kept envisioning her own play being presented on that stage. The thought made her almost giddy. *What would it take?* she wondered. *And do I even have what it takes?*

Was her play that good? And how would she ever know? She knew almost no one in the theater world. Perhaps some of her old connections could point her to someone who would at least critique the script. But when? Erik only agreed to stay a few days. And the time was flying by.

Although she was submerged in her own thoughts, she sensed that Erik was not at all bored. During intermission in the crowded lobby, they were surrounded by the elegant of New York decked in furs and satin, top hats and tails. But she had eyes for none of them. What she did see was the same pleasure and thrill reflected in Erik's face that she herself was feeling.

"You like it, don't you?" she exclaimed.

"I do." His voice held a note of surprise. "I wasn't sure at first, but I've always enjoyed a good story. We had an excellent drama team at Kendall College and I enjoyed their plays. But it was nothing compared to this."

She wanted to ask him if he thought God would approve, but she didn't dare break the spell.

That night, back in Hamptonwood, even though the hour was late, the two of them sat out on the balcony looking at the night sky and talking. Decisions must be made soon as to their future, and it was time to discuss the subject in earnest.

"Have you ever thought about Florida?" Erik asked at one point in the conversation. "There's a boom going on down there in land and buildings. New communities springing up all over the place. Surely one of those communities would need a newspaper."

Clarette's response was silence.

"And it's warm there, too," Erik added.

She thought of some of the boom towns in the Osage country that were often vacated as quickly as they were built. "Booms are so risky," she said. "It seems more luck than anything. Although the thought of a warm climate sounds nice," she added.

"I suppose you're right about being risky."

They discussed Bartlesville and the opportunities there, but Erik didn't seem ready to return to Oklahoma just yet. Several other ideas were brought up and bandied about. Again Clarette wondered if he'd thought about the job offer from Sid. Perhaps he was repulsed at the idea of staying in New York.

Finally, she could stand it no longer. Broaching it from another direction, she ventured to say, "Did you happen to notice there was an apartment for rent at Herta's place?"

He looked at her now in the semi-darkness, studying her face. "I did, but I didn't think you did."

"Why?"

"I figured if staying here were one of the options you had in mind, you'd have said something right off."

Clarette gave a little laugh. "I was waiting to see how you felt about it."

"Now aren't we a couple of swells. I can't seem to get Sid's job offer out of my mind either."

"And I've been waiting patiently for you to bring it up first." She could hardly believe this. "Erik, are you telling me you'd actually consider staying in New York?"

He nodded. "I've been thinking what a great opportunity it'd be to see how a *real* newspaper operates."

"Oh Erik!" She jumped from where she was sitting and plopped down on his lap, wrapping her arms around his neck. "And I could begin to find help with my play."

Another nod. "I thought about that, too."

"I can't believe it."

"Does the idea excite you that much?" he wanted to know.

"It excites me very much!" She grew serious a moment. "I want you to know I appreciate your concern about my play. Your caring means a lot to me."

"I guess I'm still upset about the treatment you received over the theater project back home." He shook his head. "I can't understand some folks' way of thinking. Anyway, in New York you'll have a chance to see what you can do with it."

"A chance," she said repeating the word reverently. "That's all I want. Just a chance." She kissed his cheek. "Thank you darling."

"We'll call about the apartment tomorrow."

"And call Sid?"

Erik thought a moment. "I'd better go see him in person—alone."

"That's a good idea. Sid would respect you for that."

"He's an interesting man. Think I can work with him?"

She stood to her feet, stretching and trying to stifle a yawn. "Erik Torsten, you could work with anybody," she assured him. "You're just that kind of person." She took his hand and pulled him to his feet. "Let's get some sleep. We have a lot to do in the next few days."

But long after Erik's heavy breathing sounded in the feather bed beside her, sleep had fled for Clarette. Their conversation kept playing over and over in her mind. It seemed almost too good to be true. Erik had seen the sign at the apartment, and he'd been seriously thinking about Sid's offer as well, but hesitated to say anything. Everything was turning out so perfectly. What had she ever done to deserve such a sweet husband?

———◉———

CLARETTE'S FATHER HAD left for the city by the time Erik and Clarette made their way downstairs for a late breakfast. Her mother politely came to the breakfast nook to sit with them as they ate.

Unable to contain her good news, Clarette explained their new plan while Viletta listened.

When she finished, her mother said, "For the fact that perhaps I'll be seeing you more often, I'm quite pleased." Then to Erik, "But in heaven's name, if you're going to remain in the area, why won't you consider Mr. Vanderpool's offer of employment?"

"Mother, that's not fair," Clarette protested. "Erik has a right to..."

"No, Clarette, that's all right," Erik interrupted her. "She has a legitimate question." Turning to his mother-in-law, he said, "I appreciated the offer of a job working for Mr. Vanderpool's company, but I need to do what's right for me, just as you, in years past, did what was right for you. Clarette's told me how you owned your own successful millinery shop before your marriage to Mr. Vanderpool. A commendable venture indeed. You were years ahead of your time."

Clarette smiled as she listened to Erik smoothing her mother's ruffled feathers.

"As one independent thinker to another," he continued, "I felt sure you of all people, would understand."

Mrs. Vanderpool was quiet a moment, as though thinking back. It'd been years since Clarette saw her mother's mask slip ever so slightly. "Well then," she said, rising to leave, "if your minds are made up, I can only wish you the best of luck."

Erik stood as well and reached out to shake her hand. "I accept your good wishes."

When they were alone, they mapped out the day—phone calls to place, arrangements to be made. "Once we know if we have the apartment," Clarette said, "we can call your parents and have them ship a few of our things up here." She looked up from the list she was writing. "I'll call Mr. Swinney, the landlord, right now. The apartment seems to be the place to begin."

They went into the library to use the phone there. "You'll like Mr. Swinney," she told Erik as she sat down at the secretary desk and picked up the telephone. "He's a considerate landlord."

Mr. Swinney confirmed that the apartment was indeed still available. She set a time to meet him there and so they could look at the place and possibly put down a deposit.

Then Erik took the telephone from her and called Arthur and Lillian to let them know the plans and to ask them to ship their things.

"Did they sound terribly disappointed that we're not coming back?" Clarette asked as he hung up.

"Surprisingly no. Dad seems quite pleased about the whole thing."

"What did he say?"

Erik smiled. "He said, 'Son, you'll learn a thing or two in that place.' But he didn't say if that was bad or good."

"Why it's good, of course," she said jumping up from the desk, and taking a glance at her pendant watch. "Come on. We'd better get ready and get out of here. This day's getting away from us, and we've a million things to do."

Kind old Mr. Swinney was surprised to learn that Mrs. Erik Torsten was one of his former tenants. "I thought Miss Erhardt told me you'd left for Indian Territory," he said.

"I did, Mr. Swinney. I was sent out to Oklahoma on a newspaper assignment. But now I'm back. And this is Mr. Erik Torsten, my husband."

Mr. Swinney stuck out a gnarled hand. "Did she find you out there in Oklahoma?" he asked.

"She most certainly did," Erik replied.

Mr. Swinney raised his eyebrows. "Must have been quite an assignment!" he said with a smile playing at the corners of his mouth. "Come now." He turned to lead them upstairs. "Let's have a look at this apartment, though Mrs. Torsten can tell you right now, it's clean. Anyone in Flatbush can tell you—all Mr. Swinney's apartments are clean and in good repair. I take pride in my apartment house. Great pride."

The furnished apartment was just as he promised, neat and tidy, and only a bit smaller than the space they'd had in the house in Bartlesville. The pieces of furniture, while not fancy, were durable and practical. Erik put down the deposit, and Mr. Swinney informed them they could move in any time.

That done, it was time to travel back downtown to the office of the *American*.

"Have you changed your mind about not wanting me to come along to talk with Sid?" Clarette asked as they boarded the speeding subway.

Erik shook his head. "I have not. You made the first introductions. I need to do this part alone."

Chapter 14

With the help of Clarette's instructions, Erik quickly caught on to the subway maps. It wasn't all that difficult once he understood how the streets and avenues were numbered. Although the subways were crowded and noisy, Erik was intrigued with how intricate, and yet how practical the system was. Public transportation had been of little interest back in Bartlesville, where the popularity of the automobile had nearly put their trolley system out of business.

Now that their decision to stay in New York was settled, Erik found he looked at things differently. In the not-too-distant future, he'd be boarding the underground trains on his own. The prospect wasn't as formidable as he'd first thought. In fact, the more they discussed future plans, the more pleased he became. That, plus the fact that Clarette's enthusiasm was strong enough to infect most anyone. He enjoyed watching her animation as she pointed out the different stops in an attempt to familiarize him with the layout of the city.

He'd been right all along that his wife missed New York. In fact, she probably missed it more than she was willing to admit.

When they arrived at the building which housed the *American*, he suggested she order a cup of coffee and wait for him in Fabiano's.

"Just remember," she said, giving him a quick kiss, "Sid's a kind soul beneath the gruff surface."

"I'll remember."

"And remind him this was his idea," she added.

Erik smiled at her coaching. "I don't think I'll have to remind him." He took a few steps backward from her then turned and hurried down the hallway to the elevators.

Hardly a head turned when Erik entered the noisy newsroom full of harried reporters and clacking typewriters. The area was nearly twice the size of the one he'd worked in back in Tulsa. As he had with the subway maps, he now was looking this place differently, taking careful note of each detail.

He waited to see if someone would come and ask what he wanted. When no one did, he went to Sid's door and knocked.

"What do you want?" Sid barked. "Don't just stand there!"

Erik opened the door, removing his hat as he did so.

"No need to take your hat off in this place," Sid growled. "Not a gentleman in the whole joint." He tossed a copy sheet into a basket and shook his head. "That stuff reads awful. Don't know if he's worth the time it'd take to teach him better."

Erik hesitated a moment, but Sid waved him in. "Sit down, sit down. So you decided to come back. I suppose you're looking for that job I offered."

All the confidence Erik felt coming up the elevator suddenly evaporated. This man wasn't as simple to figure out as Erik first thought. "We've decided—Clarette and I—to stay in New York for a time," Erik began. "We just put a deposit down on..."

"What do you want to do?" Sid opened his humidor, pulled out one of his cheap cigars, clipped the end and lit it. It immediately went out.

"Pardon me?"

"You want to work for me? For this newspaper?"

"Yes sir. That's why I'm here."

"Well, tell me what you want to do." The cigar was now firmly clenched in his teeth.

The gist of the conversation took Erik off guard. "I assumed I'd have to take whatever was available."

"Maybe. Maybe not." He pulled out another copy sheet and glanced at it. Looking up at Erik again he said, "Well?"

Erik sat up a little straighter. If Sid didn't really want to know he shouldn't have asked. "I'm interested in Izzy Eisenbaum and his operation. I'd like to dig into the files and learn more about him. Then I'd like to follow him around and get a few scoops on his work."

"That all?"

"No sir. But I'm not familiar enough with the city and the paper yet to know what else is available."

Sid nodded. "Good enough answer. Nobody around here cares much about following Eisenbaum."

"Why is that?"

"Like I said when youse was in here yesterday, the fellow is everywhere, like a bulldog pup. Never quits, never gives up. Works crazy oddball hours. Wears a whole peck of disguises."

Erik nodded remembering how Izzy's disguise had once fooled him. "I've seen how he works."

"You've only seen a fraction. He's got a partner working with him. Moe, they call him. Between the two of them, they've fooled a passel of bootleggers and hootchmakers."

Erik nodded, listening carefully to try to figure out what Sid was driving at.

"You want I should let you start out on Izzy?" he asked.

A couple of ideas were hatching inside Erik's head. "I'd very much like to take an assignment on Eisenbaum."

"How are you with a camera?"

"Fair."

Sid chomped his cigar and nodded. "Okay, when can you start?"

"How's next Monday?" It was Thursday, and Erik figured they'd need a couple days to get settled in.

Sid stood to his feet. "Monday's fine. Report right here at eight."

"Thanks." Erik reached out to shake Sid's hand.

Returning the handshake Sid said, "You might not be thanking me when you find out how many people in the city don't like Eisenbaum, and don't like their pictures took while they're gettin' tossed in the paddywagon."

Erik nodded. "I assumed as much."

"Consider yourself duly warned."

There wouldn't be a polite walk to the door as the editor had done yesterday when Erik and Clarette visited together. Sid was now his boss and Erik was the employee. The stocky man sat back down at the desk and began to read copy. Erik let himself out.

———— ●● ————

CLARETTE WAS OVERJOYED at Erik's good fortune. "I think Sid likes you." She hooked her arm through his as they made their way down Seventh Avenue toward the train station. "I can't believe he actually asked you what you'd like to do."

"Sure surprised me. It took me a few minutes to get my wits about me and give a solid answer."

"How do you plan to get on top of Izzy's operation? Spend a day in the morgue files?"

Erik shook his head. "I thought I'd go see him."

Clarette laughed. "Go see Izzy?"

"Sure."

"At his home?"

"Why not?"

"Well, why not indeed," Clarette quipped, marveling at her husband's creativity.

"After all, he did a great service for my buddy when he helped us get Gaven out of jail last winter. Now I'm here in the city. It's the least I can do to look him up and thank him."

"And how do you proposed to find out where he lives?"

He looked down at her smiling face. "That, my dear, is where I'll need your help."

———— ●● ————

SINCE THAT EVENING would be the last one spent with the Vanderpools for a while, Clarette felt it only right that they join her parents for dinner. Erik agreed, only if she could make sure he didn't have to spend hours in the smoking room afterward.

"Sorry, darling," she said. "I can't promise much."

Erik grit his teeth for an uncomfortable evening. And it was. The reception from Mr. Vanderpool at their future plans was open repugnance.

He warned them both of the evils of the corporate newspaper world. Then he outlined how prohibition was spawning gangster mobs who were getting into the illegal liquor business in a big way. And then reiterated his offer of a nice safe job in the nice safe garment industry.

Erik wanted to relay to him all the evils that were prevalent in the great baby state of Oklahoma, but it seemed pointless. Clarette answered him by saying, "Father, we live in a fallen world. There's not a place on earth where there's no evil."

"Perhaps not," he said, "but that's no reason for one to go courting the evil."

Seeing there was no way to win the argument, Erik gave her a look that urged her to drop the subject. But it gave him insight as to how Clarette's parents continually made her feel as though she could never please them. What a frustrating way to have to live. He didn't wonder that she spent so little time at home. Sizing up the situation, he became even more determined to support Clarette as much as he could, in every way he could.

BY THE NEXT AFTERNOON, their clothes were hanging in the plain oak wardrobe in the bedroom of their new apartment. Together they went to the market to purchased staples for the pantry. As they carried their shopping bags back to the apartment, Erik asked Clarette what she thought would be the simplest way to find Izzy's home address.

After thinking for a moment, she said, "I'd search for files containing information on Eisenbaum." She shifted the shopping bag to the other hand as they walked. "You might be able to get the information at the Bureau, but I'd suggest starting at the *American* where fewer people would ask questions."

"Good idea. I think I'll go over there this afternoon." He opened the front door of their apartment building and let her in. "You don't mind do you?"

"Not at all. I have enough to do around here. You go on." Stopping at the landing to catch her breath, she added, "I might have supper ready when you get home—even without Dovey here to help me."

"And I," he countered, "might find my way to Manhattan—even without you along to help me."

Her lilting laughter filled the hallway as he fumbled in his pocket for the key to let them in. After helping get the bags onto the small drop-leaf kitchen table, he kissed Clarette good-bye and hurried on his way downtown.

At the *American*, Erik found Sid sauntering around outside his office. The hard-nosed editor couldn't mask his surprise at seeing Erik. "Got your days mixed up? Thought you wasn't starting till Monday. It's only Friday."

"I'd like to spend a few hours in the morgue. Any objections?"

"Naw. No objections. Hold on and I'll get somebody to show you around. They're down on seventh floor." Looking around, Sid called across the room. "Hey, Maxwell. Come here a sec."

Erik immediately recognized the name. Hank Maxwell was the *rival* she and Herta mentioned. He'd given Clarette a great deal of trouble when she worked for Sid, but that certainly gave Erik no reason to dislike the man. After all, Erik too had been guilty of being rude to Clarette when she first barged into the *Tulsa World*.

Maxwell was a slender man of medium build, about half-a-head shorter than Erik. His hat sat precariously on the back of his head and a cigarette was tucked behind one ear, and pencil tucked behind the other. "You call me, Boss?"

"Maxwell, this here's Erik Torsten. I'm starting him out Monday in Carlisle's old spot. Take him down and show him the morgue. He wants to rummage a while."

Maxwell studied Erik intently. The seasoned reporter probably didn't miss a thing. "He starts Monday? This is Friday."

"Brilliant thinking, Maxwell. Now step on it, will you? I want that story you're working on, pronto!"

Maxwell was now miffed. "Let him show himself down to seventh. He's old enough to ride the elevator without an escort."

"I'm not asking, Maxwell, I'm telling," came Sid's no-nonsense reply.

The scene made Erik somewhat uncomfortable, but he wanted in those files so kept quiet.

Still grumbling under his breath, Maxwell marched toward the newsroom door. "Come on," he said to Erik motioning him to follow.

"You talk funny," Maxwell said as they rode the elevator down. "You from around here?"

"Oklahoma."

"That right? I knew a reporter from here who went to Tulsa for a story last year."

"Could her name be Clarette Fortier?"

Maxwell shoved the hat further back on his head. "You know her?"

"I married her."

"Seventh floor," announced the elevator operator, holding the metal grating open. Hank Maxwell just stood there and stared at Erik. "For crying out loud."

"Seventh Floor," the operator repeated, prompting Hank to disembark. He pointed down the hall. "The morgue's this way," he said.

"Somebody told me Miss Fortier was back for a visit. I mean, Mrs...
What was it? Torsten?"

Erik nodded, following Maxwell in the door to the room where
wooden file cabinets stood in rows like miniature fortresses.

"I'll be fine, Maxwell," Erik stuck out his hand. "You can get back to
your deadline. Thanks for the escort," he added using Hank's choice of
words.

Hank smiled and returned the handshake. "Tell me what you're
looking for and maybe I can help." He leaned an elbow against a file as
though he suddenly had all the time in the world.

"Nothing in particular," Erik answered hedging as best he could.
Hank seemed a nice enough fellow, but why push it? "I'm new,
remember? I've got a lot to learn."

"Yeah, you sure do." Erik couldn't miss the edge of sarcasm in the
remark. With a broad sweep of his arm, Hank said, "You could spend
years in here and never read it all."

But Erik refused to be moved. He'd met Maxwell's kind in the
Army—suspicious, wary, keeping close watch on anyone who might
move into his territory.

"An hour or two a day in here should prove very profitable," Erik
said quietly and still did not move.

Presently, Hank seemed to get the message that Erik wasn't talking,
and he stepped toward the door. "I know this city inside out," he said,
giving Erik a friendly smile. "Be sure to let me know if you need
anything. I'd be more than happy to help any way I can."

Erik gave a little salute. "I'll do it." He watched the man's shadow
move down the hall through the frosted windows of the morgue.
Contented that Hank was truly gone, Erik began digging in the files for
the name of Eisenbaum and he wasn't disappointed. The file was thick
and running over.

He carefully studied the rotogravures of the short, heavyset federal
agent, with the friendly, almost childlike face. Erik shook his head in

amazement. This man, who'd never taken a bribe and never carried a weapon, held the record of more arrests than any other agent in the Federal Prohibition Bureau. His outlandish comic-opera disguises had fooled even the best. From the clippings, Erik learned that the *American* hadn't had many scoops on Izzy, who'd served as an agent almost since the onset of prohibition two years ago. And Izzy's address and phone number were right there in the file.

Tomorrow he and Clarette would pay the Eisenbaums a little social visit.

Chapter 15

The Lower East Side where the Eisenbaum's flat was located, was an older neighborhood with nondescript brown tenement buildings lining the narrow streets. From the back seat of the taxicab, Clarette studied the few shade trees that struggled to survive in the space between the sidewalks and the street. Beneath the trees on the sidewalks and scraggly lawns, bunches of noisy children played skip rope, hopscotch, and ball and jacks.

When the cabbie pulled to a stop at the correct address on East Fourth, Erik handed him a bill and said, "Keep the change, buddy," before helping Clarette out onto the curb.

"What a great idea," she told him as they walked up the sidewalk to the front stoop. "I'm proud of you, my dear."

"Compliments may be premature at this stage. All this might come to nothing."

Several boys on their knees in the dirt were engrossed in a heated game of marbles. "Eisenbaums live here?" Erik asked.

"Fifth floor," one replied without looking up.

Erik had placed a call to Mr. Eisenbaum the evening before, but his wife said he was out. When Erik explained who they were and where they'd come from, she insisted they come over the next morning. Clarette hoped Izzy would be there.

Mrs. Eisenbaum was nearly as short and round as her husband, with a wide smile and a happy rosy-cheeked face. Cordially, she invited them in to the crowded, but extremely neat and clean flat. Erik had told Clarette that there were four little Eisenbaums, all of whom must have been outside playing since all was quiet.

"Beulah," she told them as introductions were made. "My name's Beulah, and you can call me that."

Just as she invited them to sit down on the davenport, which was flanked by a mahogany Victrola, Izzy came out from a back bedroom.

"Would you just look," he said smiling. "The Swede who's the only person ever to get the drop on this little agent." He stepped over to Erik, who towered over him, and happily pumped his hand. "Mama, this is the one I told you about in the woods in Oklahoma."

Beulah laughed. "So many stories you tell, you think I should have them straight? But it does not matter." She wiped her hands on her blue checkered apron. "I get us something to eat."

"May I help?" Clarette offered.

Beulah shook her head and shooed with her hands. "You go now. Sit down. You visit."

Amidst Beulah's bustling about, Erik was able to explain to Izzy that they were now living in New York, and that he was working at the *American*.

"Your work fascinates me," Erik said to Izzy. "Perhaps it's the reporter part of me, but I'd like to know more. Why do most of the stories on your raids appear long after the fact?"

A chuckle came from deep within Izzy's ample midsection. "You want I should tell you the truth?"

Erik nodded. "I wouldn't have asked otherwise."

"Lazy. Reporters, they can't keep up with me. I have arrests made some mornings before some agents are out of bed almost. Most definitely before reporters are out of bed."

Clarette watched Erik's face. She knew he'd surmised as much. "What's the best way to get a scoop on a big bust?"

"No stroke of genius needed. Just follow along."

Erik paused a moment to accept from Beulah a china plate holding a thick slice of bread with a golden crust. "Thank you, Beulah." Then to Izzy, "I know you can't tell me ahead of time where you're going, but can you tell me a strategic time and place?"

Izzy pointed out their front window. "Down there at five-thirty Monday morning."

"I can follow you in a cab?"

Izzy chuckled again. "I can't stop you."

Clarette felt her pulse quicken. Erik was on to something. She had no doubt his zeal and resourcefulness would make a great impact on Sid. Her husband would quickly become an indispensable asset to the big city newspaper. She could hardly contain her pride and her excitement.

———◉———

THEY RETURNED TO HERTA'S church the following Sunday, only now everything was different. There was no hurry and so following the service they accepted the invitation to eat dinner at the home of Pastor Bren Roswald and his wife, Adele. Their cozy bungalow was situated directly behind the church building. The couple exuded warmth and friendliness and Clarette quickly relaxed in their home and in their presence.

Over a dinner of pot roast and boiled vegetables, the couple asked polite questions in an effort to get to know more about Erik and Clarette. The questions, Clarette sensed, were not prying, but rather stemmed from a genuine interest.

The Roswalds had lost a son in the war, and their daughter and her family were missionaries in India. However, the older couple spent no time lamenting over possible loneliness, but instead threw themselves into the work of the church with a robust vigor.

Later that afternoon on their way home, Clarette could tell that Erik, too, was impressed with the church. "We don't need to make a firm decision right away," he told her. "But I'm comfortable attending there until the Lord shows us differently."

She agreed completely.

It was that afternoon when Clarette realized she'd not talked to Grandmother Vanderpool to tell her they were staying in the city. Since their phone had not yet been installed, she went upstairs to borrow Herta's.

Clarette had assumed her grandmother would be overjoyed at their decision. But there was no note of excitement in the older woman's voice when she heard the news. The unexpected response both startled and confused Clarette.

"What is it?" Clarette wanted to know. "Aren't you pleased that you'll be seeing me more often? I'll be right here close."

"Of course, my dear. You know how I love to see you and be with you."

"And this will give you a chance to know Erik better."

"Yes that's true," she answered. But the reservation still sounded in her voice.

"What's wrong? I was so sure you'd be thrilled for both of us. I'll have a chance now to possibly find an agent to help me sell my script as well."

She had told her grandmother all about the situation with Exa Belle and the judgmental women at First Church. Now that she was out of their clutches, she was free to pursue her passion.

"Yes, I know all that and I'm happy for you."

"Then will you please tell me what's bothering you?"

There was a heavy pause. "Clarette, New York City is a hard and cruel taskmaster. Erik is so sweet and so good, and the wolves that lurk here are ravenous."

Clarette stiffened at this remark. "And what makes you think Indian Territory is clean and innocent? Why, you can't possibly imagine the wild things that go on out there. Erik grew up right in the midst of all of it—Klan activities, greedy oil men, ruthless roustabouts..."

"I know, Clarette. But he knew the rules there; Erik has no New York street savvy. I very much fear he'll be eaten alive."

"Why that's the silliest thing I've ever heard. You make him sound like he's a baby. This man survived the war!"

"I may be wrong, Clarette. I pray that I am. But make sure the two of you pray about the details. And look deep inside to examine your own motives."

"Now what's that supposed to mean? I can hardly believe I'm hearing you say these things. You sound almost as bad as Exa Belle." Clarette's heart pounded heavy inside her chest. How could her beloved grandmother be so wrong about things? She took a deep breath. "Look, I'm sorry. I didn't mean to lash out. But you'll just have to trust our judgment in this. We both feel we're doing exactly what God has called us to do."

"Very well, Clarette. Just keep in mind what I've said. Now I hope you'll plan to come over for tea one afternoon very soon. I promise I'll not harp."

"I'll be downtown most every day next week. I'll call first."

When she got off the phone, she was embarrassed to realize that in the small apartment, her every word had been overheard. As she went out to the kitchen, Herta looked at her with concern. "Everything is all right?"

"I'm not sure."

"Want to talk about it?"

She hated to burden anyone with her problems. "It's nothing really. Just a bit of a misunderstanding with Grandmother." She gave a little laugh. "She seems to think this town will eat Erik alive."

"You've always known your grandmother to be very wise."

"Oh no," Clarette said in exasperation. "Don't tell me you agree with her."

"Did I say I agree with her sentiments? I simply remind you that she is a wise lady."

"You don't even know her," Clarette snapped back, hating her tone but feeling helpless to cap her mounting anger.

"I only know she's the one you have looked to for support for all these years."

"That doesn't mean she's always right about everything."

"What is it that's making you so upset, Clarette?"

"I'm not upset!" She stepped to the door and opened it. "I'll talk to you later when you make more sense." Closing the door after her, she fought the urge to slam it. Taking a couple steps down the hall, she turned and walked back to Herta's door. Sticking her head in, she said, "And thanks for letting me borrow the telephone."

"Of course. Anytime."

When she went back to her own apartment, Erik was taking a nap on the davenport. That was good. She'd have time to cool her anger.

Anger. She could hardly believe it. Even before she became a Christian, she seldom had outbursts of anger. But how infuriating to have her grandmother try to tell her what was best for her. She certainly had no intention of telling Erik what Grandmother Vanderpool said. There was no sense in planting bad seeds of thoughts in his mind. She shook her head. How could New York City be any worse that the nightmare existence her husband endured on the Western Front?

She took out her Underwood and set it up on the kitchen table. While Erik slept, she worked on the revisions to her play script. Working on her play never failed to lift her spirits.

———◦———

ERIK WAS UP AND READY to go out the door by four-thirty Monday morning. With Clarette's help the evening before, he knew to take the subway as far as Delancey Street. From there he'd take a cab to Eisenbaum's tenement row, then wait for Izzy.

He didn't have to wait long. At five-thirty sharp, Izzy came down the front stoop wearing the tweed hat and rough work clothes of a common factory laborer. He climbed into the battered Model T provided by the bureau, and with not a glance in Erik's direction, drove off.

Erik instructed the cabbie to follow at a good distance. When Izzy stopped at a storefront near a factory in the waterfront district, Erik exited his taxicab a couple blocks away. Since he was armed with his camera, he knew he'd look fairly conspicuous.

Making his way down the street in closer proximity, he found an empty doorway and waited. Within fifteen minutes, police paddy wagons were pulling up out front and several well-dressed men were being arrested and loaded in. Erik stepped right up, taking photos and asking questions. One good shot was of the uniformed policeman hooking a padlock on the door and posting the "closed" sign on the door.

With so many people around, he was careful not to act as though he knew Izzy, other than as the famous prohibition sleuth. In bits and pieces, he learned that the proprietor never suspected that a federal agent might be working the "establishments" before the first factory whistle blew. Once again, Izzy's innocent face and believable disguise foiled the dealers.

"This was a place where no other agent had been able to buy a drink," Izzy said, as Erik furiously scribbled notes. Then Izzy's face wreathed in a wide smile. "But they served me right and proper."

Pulling open his coat, he showed Erik the small funnel which fit in his pocket and led to a flask concealed in the lining of his coat. "This is how I confiscate the goods," he said with a note of pride. "They serve me; I pour the evidence in here. Works every time."

At seven-thirty, Erik strode into the newsroom at the *American*. Maxwell saw him come in and sauntered up. "Hey cowboy. Ready for your first day at work in the big city?"

"Almost ready, Maxwell." He jerked his head toward the editor's office. "Is Sid in?"

"He's in there. Probably got your first assignment ready and waiting. If you're lucky, you might get to cover the tea being held by the Women's Christian Temperance Union."

A few other reporters who were milling about, snickered at the remark. Realizing he had an audience, Maxwell waved toward Erik's camera and film case which was slung over his shoulder. "With all that equipment, you should be able to grab some real good shots of all them fat ladies sipping tea and nibbling crumpets."

More snickers.

Erik smiled, tipped his hat, and walked to Sid's office. In answer to the growl coming from the other side, he let himself in.

"Torsten," Sid said, looking up. "Good to see you. I've been thinking about what you said about Eisenbaum. I think I'll let you have a go at it."

"I was hoping you'd say that. I scooped a raid on a speakeasy near the docks first thing this morning. A place the feds have been trying to shut down for weeks." He held up a box of exposed film then placed it on the editor's desk. "Here're the shots I took, not only of those caught with the goods, but of owners and customers being loaded up and taken away."

Sid nearly dropped his cigar.

Chapter 16

Clarette's bound play script lay heavy and conspicuous in her lap as she sat waiting in the crowded anteroom. Others in the room were obviously out-of-work performers looking for their big break. She was the only one holding a script. In her purse was a dog-eared sheet of paper listing names and addresses of play producers in the city, several of which had dark lines drawn through them.

She'd made her way from the office of one producer to another for three days with absolutely no luck. Adjusting the script and smoothing wrinkles from her blue voile skirt, she held her head erect, crossed her legs primly at the ankles, and tucked them slightly back as she'd been taught years ago at Miss Damerow's Preparatory High School. She refused to allow the discouragement she was feeling to show in her face or her actions.

At one end of the small room a young lady with elegant finger-waves, and way too much lip rouge, shuffled papers on her desk, answered phone calls, and pecked away at the typewriter. A recent graduate of secretarial school, Clarette surmised silently. Behind the girl was a door with a frosted-paned window with the words, "Granville Productions," scrolled in large black letters.

To her left two men were talking in low tones. "I'd heard," said one, "that the flickers was draining off all the extra actors in New York and transplanting them to Hollywood. But I still can't find work. What do you think?"

The other man gave a snort. "I don't know about that, but the fact is the flickers are taking all the audiences away from the theaters. Another one up on Fifty-Third closed just last week."

They shook their heads in a united lament over the loss of the Broadway Theater, but Clarette didn't believe a word of it. Losers always talked that way, and she refused to join them. The theater would always be there no matter how many magnificent moving picture theaters opened up on Broadway, or anywhere else for that matter.

The frosted-paned door opened and closed with great rapidity as many people came and went, until at last her name was called. She took a little breath and stood to her feet. The young red-lipped secretary eyed the script in Clarette's hand and raised her painted eyebrows, then opened the door to the office.

Mr. Granville's office was not large, but every wall was studded with photographs of the hit plays he'd produced on Broadway—which was, as Clarette's research had revealed, a goodly number. The tall bare windows behind the producer's desk presented a view of red brick wall and a metal fire escape.

None of the producers she'd seen so far had been friendly, and Mr. Granville was no different. "What's your line?" he demanded not looking up from the stack of papers on his cluttered desk.

"I beg your pardon?" She wasn't sure whether to sit down, or wait to be asked.

He looked up now and Clarette could better see his small close-set eyes which squinted at her. "Your line, lady? What do you do?"

She hesitated. Why couldn't they at least be cordial? "I'm a playwright," she said keeping her voice as even as possible.

"Who sent you?"

Again she was forced to hesitate. What should she say? "No one sent me. That is..."

"How'd you know to come here?"

Becoming impatient with his cold demeanor, she said, "Sir, I've a play script here. May I leave a copy with you to review?"

He shook his head. "I don't take no scripts from anyone but the agents I know."

"Don't you miss a lot of good work that way?"

He waved his pencil at the photos on the wall. "Does it look like I've missed much?"

She had to admit, it didn't look that way at all.

"Look ma'am, I'm busy. Thanks for coming by." He pushed a button on the black box on his desk. "Miss Fry, please send the next one in."

There was nothing she could do but leave. Out on the sidewalk once again, she drew the wrinkled list from her purse and looked at the next name. The afternoon sun had grown quite warm, and her feet throbbed.

Every place she went, it was the same thing. Either they weren't in the market for a script, wouldn't take time to read a new script, or told her to get an agent. Never had she imagined it would be so difficult just to get a reading. To have the play turned down was one thing, to never have it looked at was quite another. Surely there was some way to break in.

Taking a rest for a moment, she stepped inside a drug store to order a cool lime phosphate. She chose a small table near the magazine racks. While sipping the tangy drink she noticed a copy of *Mosaics* magazine on the shelf. She'd written articles for *Mosaics* last year while she lived in Tulsa. The editor, Romney Kimbell, had been a classmate of hers at Columbia University when she attended there. She'd not even thought about him or the magazine since arriving back in the city. Reaching for the magazine, she flipped to the masthead which gave the address on West Thirty-Fifth. Not far.

She tucked the magazine back in its proper place, finished the last of the phosphate and ignoring her throbbing feet, walked back down Seventh Avenue. Perhaps Romney knew something about the world of Broadway. And if not, perhaps he had an assignment or two she could take.

Many of the older buildings in downtown Manhattan were still without elevators, and Clarette had lost track of the flights of stairs her tired feet had scaled in the past few days. The directory in the lobby listed the editorial offices of *Mosaics* on fifth floor.

"Couldn't have been on second," she muttered as she made her way to the stairwell.

Romney was more than pleased to see her—a refreshing change from the cold rebuffs she'd endured lately. Romney had changed little from their college days—his narrow face now sported a small neat mustache and the black round-rimmed glasses lent a studious air. He certainly looked the part of an editor.

They exchanged pleasantries as he thanked her again for the insightful articles she'd written for them regarding the aftermath of the Tulsa race riot.

"What occupies your time since you've come back to New York?" he wanted to know. "Besides being a housewife, that is."

Clarette almost laughed out loud. She'd had precious little time to be a housewife. Some of the parcels and boxes which Erik's mother had shipped from Bartlesville were still stacked in a corner of the bedroom. Some nights Erik didn't arrive home until late. As Sid was learning to trust him with ever bigger scoops, he was being sent out to tail Izzy and other agents almost daily

However, since Romney had politely asked, she took the opportunity to explain about her script—toning down the fact that she'd received nothing but rejections. When she asked him if he knew anything about agents who worked with Broadway producers, he shook his head. "That's way out of my territory," he told her.

"I thought as much."

"However," he added quickly, "there's a speakeasy in the basement of the Allmont Hotel where writers and show people gather to enjoy what bubbly they can obtain. I've gone there a time or two myself. Lots of deals are made there."

A speakeasy. There was a time, not too long ago, when she would have hurried right down to the Allmont to see what was happening. But now it was out of the question.

"You can't sit home and expect agents to come to you," Romney said into the silence. "Get around town, Clarette. A few parties, a few speakeasies on a Saturday night, and before long you'll know everyone who is anyone."

Something inside of her wanted to explain to him that she was a Christian now, but *how* to say it wasn't quite clear.

Romney pulled open a side desk drawer. "I just happened to think. Here's the card of a friend of mine who's done some bit parts on Broadway. Maybe he knows of an agent."

As he stood up to hand her the card, she knew it was time to make her exit. Back out on the street, she realized she'd not even asked Romney if he had any assignments. Oh well, she could call him tomorrow.

Making her way to a phone booth, she gave the operator the number printed on the business card. The name on the card was Thomas Netzer, and thankfully, it was Mr. Netzer who answered the ring. Getting right to the point, she told him that Romney suggested she call, and then explained about her script. "Romney thought you might know of an agent who could help me," she said.

His reply held a note of disbelief. "Lady, I don't mean to be impolite, but are you blind? Have you not seen all the moving picture theaters around town—some right there on Broadway? Mr. and Mrs. America are choosing their entertainment differently these days. Market's not too keen for plays. The ball park's too crowded, Mrs. Torsten," he said tersely. "That means some players need to stay home."

Clarette didn't like his patronizing tone one bit. "But good plays will always be needed," she insisted. "Don't you agree?"

"Sure, sure. Good plays—from known playwrights."

Clarette attempted to swallow her mounting anger. She'd called to ask for the name of an agent, not for a report on the climate of Broadway. "You have a right to your opinion, Mr. Netzer, and I have a right to mine. Do you or do you not know of an agent I might contact?"

"None that would handle an unknown. And certainly none that would handle an unknown who also happens to be a dame."

Steeling herself against his crass remark, she thanked Mr. Thomas Netzer and rang off.

The nerve. She wished she could have told him the number of times she'd been published, plus the fact that she'd been a reporter for the *American* right alongside a number of men.

The subway ride toward Brooklyn late that afternoon at least gave her feet a brief rest. As the train rumbled along, she thought about her relationship with Sid Epstein. That man knew everyone in New York. He'd surely know of a good agent. But since he was now Erik's boss, it didn't seem right to contact him. She tried to stay out of Erik's work as much as possible. Which was quite different than when they worked on the *Courier* and were together almost every minute of every day. Though she couldn't say she missed the *Courier*, she did miss the hours working alongside Erik.

She considered what Romney had said about the speakeasy where writers and artists gathered. How wrong would it be to stop in a few times if she never drank anything? Another gray area. How was a person ever supposed to know what God wanted?

Romney was right about one thing, she needed to get out and meet others in the theater business if she ever hoped to make a connection. And people like Thomas Netzer were no help at all.

Chapter 17

Sweat trickled down Erik's back and face as he sat on the steps of an abandoned building waiting. Pulling an old handkerchief from his pocket he mopped at his face. He'd thought there could be nothing hotter than July in Oklahoma, but that's because he'd never experienced summer heat in a city like New York. Smelly garbage and rubbish filled every alley way. Horse droppings from the many drays only added to the stench. There was an indescribable closeness about it all. Sometimes Erik felt as though he were strangling on the constrictions. The only other time he'd felt that way was the short time he'd spent in the deep trenches in France during the war.

For two long days he'd hung around this neighborhood near the lower East Side docks. Izzy was in a room upstairs waiting as well. Taking a lesson from the prohibition sleuth, Erik had dressed in old clothes in order to remain inconspicuous. He tried to keep moving around, sometimes sitting in the doorway, sometimes down the street sitting in a sandwich shop, sometimes sitting under a shade tree in a nearby vacant lot.

Across the street and down a few doors, stood the offices and warehouse of a wholesale olive oil company. Izzy suspected they were packaging more than virgin olive oil. Though Izzy was seldom wrong, Erik was beginning to doubt in this case.

He'd called Sid early that morning to ask if he should stay on Izzy's heels even though it meant another day of waiting. "Give it one more day," Sid told him. "If he busts this one, it'll definitely be a front-pager. Only the big boys would run an operation so big they'd have to use tank trucks."

Erik agreed. Steel tanks intended for olive oil could ship an awful lot of whiskey.

Ever since Erik made his first scoop, Sid decided to keep him working on the bigger busts that were taking place almost daily in the city.

"Won't people get tired of all this?" Erik asked Sid at one point. He was concerned about the sameness of it all.

Sid just waved his hand and though to dispel the thought. "Naw. Our readers love this stuff. Them that's dry are laughing to see the places closed down. Them that's wet are laughing that someone got caught besides them. Everybody's happy!

"Besides," he added, "this roll won't last forever. Sooner or later the feds are gonna get sick of this feisty little agent besting all their other agents. We'll milk this for as long as we can. Face it, Torsten, Izzy makes good copy, and you've got the nose to follow him."

When he first started, Erik was thrilled to be making the breaking scoops day after day. Seeing his stories on the front page was quite a kick. But as the summer wore on, the futility of it all became more and more apparent. No one, but no one, was going to stop the flow of liquor. Not in New York, not on the Mexican border, not on the Canadian border, not in the thousands of hidden speakeasies, and not in the bathtubs of nearly every flat and apartment in America.

What he first saw as great strides in stopping the lawlessness, he now saw as petty games. And since Sid seemed to think Erik could handle the assignments single handedly, it spelled longs days and late hours. Two times he'd even worked on Sunday, something he'd never done before in his life. He couldn't remember the last time he and Clarette had had a leisurely prayer time together.

Stretching his long legs, he stood to his feet and strolled around to the back of the building just to get the kinks out of his muscles.

A few days ago, Erik had photographed the hate-filled eyes of Vannie Higgins and Big Frenchy DeMange when they were

inadvertently caught red-handed in a bust. Usually the big boys stayed
clear of the locations of rum row, preferring to conduct their business
from high atop elegant penthouse suites. Sid was quite elated over that
story and the photos, but Erik couldn't get those hate-filled eyes out of
his mind.

Izzy and Moe both seemed to bask in the publicity. Although Erik
never talked to the agents, and never made contact with them, often
one or the other would pass Erik a note, or make a quick phone call to
Erik's house giving him little tips. It made Erik's job a cinch.

Panhandlers and the down-and-out frequented this dingy
neighborhood, but today, thankfully, there was no one else around.
Following Izzy not only familiarized Erik with the layout of the
metropolis, it also gave him a glimpse into the sordid squalor of the
back streets of New York.

If it weren't for Clarette moving closer and closer to having her play
accepted, he'd call it quits and leave. It grieved him to see her working
so hard, and becoming so discouraged. Recently, he'd asked around the
newsroom for the name of an agent. Hank, who'd turned into a pretty
friendly guy, promised to keep his eyes and ears open.

Suddenly there was a tap on the window above him. Izzy's short
round frame was there peering down. He motioned for Erik to fetch
his camera. Finally. He'd be glad to get out of this place.

While he'd been waiting, he kept his camera and film case hidden
in an old crate he'd found behind the building. Carefully, he pulled it
out, readied it, and waited. Peeking out from behind the building, he
saw Izzy walking nonchalantly down the street toward where a shiny
new tanker truck had just pulled up to a loading dock. Izzy's trained
eye, watching from his window loft in the vacant building, had
obviously ascertained that the liquid being transported was not olive
oil.

Izzy, who never carried a weapon, would as always, calmly walk in, show his badge and make a simple arrest. Usually he called police headquarters right from the establishment he was shutting down.

In no time, Erik had the full story and photos. Sid was right—it was one of the biggest busts Erik had ever witnessed. Before he left, Izzy slipped him a note that let him know that Moe was downtown moving in on a bust.

Erik sighed as he made his way out of the neighborhood to find a taxi. Should he snag the story, or just go on back to the newsroom and call it a day?

———◉———

CLARETTE WAS ELATED that a producer now held a copy of her script. While it wasn't a go-ahead, at least she was further ahead than she'd been before. Daily she struggled with discouragement, but doggedly she pressed on. Each day the sidewalks were hotter and more oppressive than the day before. It was difficult to maintain a fresh appearance when she felt wilted before ten in the morning.

Today she was to have tea with Grandmother Vanderpool at four. That gave her something to look forward to. Grandmother's elegant Madison Avenue apartment overlooking Central Park would be cool and refreshing.

While Clarette had been given the names of two different agents in the past few weeks, neither of them would give her the time of day. Much as she hated to admit it, Mr. Netzer's statement was true. Times in the theater were very tight.

During the morning hours she did the usual, making stops at the various offices of producers. But this afternoon she had an actual appointment with one of the producers who had previously asked to see the script. She couldn't even allow herself to hope...

After a quick sandwich and coffee at the automat, she hurried toward the office of Mr. Elmo Rambova. While Mr. Rambova was not as well known as many of the other producers in New York, Clarette couldn't afford to pass up an opportunity.

By now, every office looked much like the one before. The gangly long-armed Rambova had a horsey expression with a long nose and wide smile. In spite of his not-so-handsome appearance, Clarette was thankful for his smile. He was thumbing through her manuscript as she walked in which immediately gave her a shot of hope.

Pointing her to a chair, he said, "Good to see you again, Mrs. Torsten. Please sit down."

Working to control her voice, she thanked him for the appointment and for taking the time to read the script.

"Well," he said, "I haven't exactly read all of it. I did read the first act and a bit of the ending."

"And?"

He gave a shrug. "It's pretty well written." He lay the script down on the desk. "But I'm trying to stay with the established playwrights I know. The way things are right now, I can't afford the risk."

Clarette felt the air go out of her.

"What you need Mrs. Torsten is some experience under your belt, or a hard-working agent who really believes in your stuff."

"But I have experience," she started. "I've been published in..."

"You told me the last time you were here, but that, Mrs. Torsten, is not the theater. In spite of all the money floating around the city these days, it's pretty tight in the theater circles."

"So I've heard."

"You heard right then." Handing her the script, he added, "There are some producers doing more shows outside the city. Perhaps you should look for something in Philadelphia or a smaller city."

She nodded. There was nothing left to say. Politely she thanked him again for his time and let herself out, marveling at the crowd still waiting in the stuffy anteroom. Some were becoming familiar faces to her.

"Maybe it's time to throw in the towel," she muttered to herself as she walked back down several flights of stairs. Fishing around in her bag for a trolley token, she pulled out the card of the speakeasy Romney had told her about. She thought sure she'd thrown that thing away.

Coming out into the bright sunshine she realized she was on upper Broadway, not far from the place stated on the card: *148 East Fifty-Sixth Street.* A quick glance at her watch told her there was time before she was due at Grandmother Vanderpool's. What could it hurt?

"If your heart condemns you not..." she remembered Dovey saying. There was nothing about a speakeasy to condemn her. Romney said she needed to get out and meet people, and that's just what she would do.

Once her mind was made up, her steps quickened as she hurried up Broadway. Romney said one card could get a person into most any place in town. But if this was where the writers congregated, then this was where she needed to be.

The Allmont Hotel was a stone building with ornate wrought-iron grillwork around the windows. Flanking a long green canopy were two sets of stairs that went up into the building. Beneath the narrow canopy was a stairway that went down.

Hesitating only a moment, she chose the center entry remembering that Romney said it was in the basement. There, behind an iron grillwork outer door, was an inner wooden door with a small window. Fighting down her nervousness, she rang the bell. A sliding panel on the window flew open startling her. All she could see was pair of unfriendly eyes staring at her.

"Who sentcha?"

Clarette's mind drew a blank. "Romney. Uh, Romney Kimball."

"Never heard of him."

Then she remembered the card. "Here," she said, holding it up so he could see. Her fingers were trembling.

The small window slid shut. She stood frozen, not knowing if she'd been admitted or turned away. Just as she decided it was the latter, both doors were opened and she was escorted inside. The long entry hall led to yet another door which opened onto a dim and crowded, but nicely furnished, club room. Oriental carpets felt soft beneath her feet. Men and women alike sat around the heavy walnut tables in tight little groups. Who would have ever thought this many people were hidden away down here in the daytime hours. She was mystified.

A lady dressed in a raspberry-colored fringed flapper dress and reeking of flowery perfume came up to her and asked if she had a preference of the bar or a table.

"A table's fine."

"Right this way."

Once seated, Clarette felt a growing sense of panic. Whatever made her think she could just walk in here and pretend she frequented these places daily?

"What'll you have?" The lady asked. When Clarette hesitated, the lady said, "This your first time here? Not to worry, honey, there's nothing you want that we don't have. From bourbon to scotch to gin, we have it all. And the best too. None of that weak alky stuff made in a rusty barrel. Most of our ladies take a liking to the Burnett's White Satin. Or you might like the Highland Cream."

"Well, I..." How had she gotten herself into this mess?

"Ah, short on cash?" The lady leaned down bringing her cloud of flowery fragrance with her. "Can I take you to that table over there?" She pointed to the corner where several young men were seated at a large round table, enjoying a lively discussion. "The gentlemen are always ready to put up for a lady's drink."

"No! That is, I think..." Clarette jumped up. "How silly of me. I just remembered I have an appointment." She grabbed her bag from off the table. "Did you ever do that?" She was backing away from the table, from the lady, from the thick cloud of perfume. "Did you ever completely forget you had someplace else to be?"

Ignoring the lady's puzzled expression, she hurried back out the way she came, down the long hall past the man at the door who let her out. The clatter of the iron grill closing behind her sent a cold shiver up her spine.

Heart still pounding, she walked quickly to the corner and crossed the street to wait for the next trolley to take her to Madison Avenue and Grandmother's place.

Her wait was short, as the trolley soon came clanging down the tracks and stopped. Stepping up, she dropped her token in the slot just as a wild commotion broke out across the street. Pushing down the aisle to find a window seat, she stared in horror as she saw police paddy wagons pulling up to the Allmont Hotel and uniformed officers piling out and converging beneath the long green canopy. The trolley pulled out, causing her to crane her neck to look back. As she did, she saw Erik jump out of a taxi, lift up the heavy Graflex camera, and start snapping photos.

Clarette pressed her head against the window and wondered if she were going to faint or throw up. Or both.

Chapter 18

"Hey Torsten!"

Erik glanced up from his typewriter to see Hank coming across the newsroom toward him.

"I've been doing just what you asked me to do, and I think I've found an agent for the little lady."

Erik straightened his shoulders and popped a knuckle or two. "That's great news, Maxwell. Is the guy on the up and up? I mean, does he know his business?"

Maxwell perched himself on a corner of Erik's desk. "Would I tell you about someone who's not on the up and up?" He reached over, slapped Erik's shoulder and gave a friendly grin. "This agent ain't like all the rest of them lazy bums your wife's been talking to. This guy—Lenny Lepke's his name—says he's reading everything. 'This is the time to strike,' Lenny tells me, 'when everybody else is bellyaching about a downturn.'" Maxwell pulled a card from inside his coat pocket. "He sounds like a go-getter to me, but maybe you just want to think about it." He waved the card and smiled.

Erik shook his head. "I don't need to think about it. Clarette's definitely due a break. She amazes me with her determination. I swear she's set foot on the doorstep of nearly every producer in New York. She never gives up."

"Determined. That defines your little lady to a fare-thee-well." He bent the card double between his fingers and flipped it in the air, forcing Erik to reach out to catch it. "You two are sorta alike in that respect," he added.

Erik mulled the remark for a moment. "Yeah, I guess you could say that."

After working with Hank all these weeks, Erik was still puzzled by the man. At first, he was sure Hank had it in for him, which kept Erik wary and at bay. But when nothing materialized he was forced to assume he'd been badly mistaken. And now this. If this Lepke guy worked out, Erik would have to admit he'd been more than wrong about Hank Maxwell.

After Hank had gone back to his own desk, Erik studied the card. He'd become increasingly concerned about Clarette and her relentless search. In his estimation, she was putting too much store by this play being produced. And especially being produced on Broadway. But what could he say? He hated to discourage her.

A recent letter from his parents had upset both of them as Lillian described in great detail the gala ground-breaking ceremony for the new community theater in Bartlesville.

He saw the hurt register on Clarette's face as she read the letter. "My theater," she muttered half in disbelief. Looking up at him she'd said, "This theater was supposed to be so sinful. So, why's your mother describing it as though it were some important event?"

Erik had no answer for her. In fact, it made him angry as well. All he could do was hold her and try to comfort her in her pain and confusion. Perhaps that was why the play was so important to her. Perhaps there something inside her wanting to *show* the whole world she could do it.

He looked at the card again, picked up the phone and jiggled the receiver to get the operator. Since it was nearly six o'clock, he didn't really expect an answer. But suddenly on the other end a man's voice answered, "Lepke Agency, Lenny speaking."

Ah. Perhaps the answer was on its way. Briefly, Erik explained to Lenny Lepke about Clarette's play and that he'd gotten Lenny's name and number from Hank Maxwell at the *American*. He also added that whatever came of this, he didn't want Clarette to know he'd placed the call.

The agent seemed congenial and willing to cooperate. "Has anyone in town actually read the script?" he wanted to know.

Erik paused a moment. "One producer took the script and read it."

"You know his name?"

Erik thought a minute. "Rambova," he said. "Elmo Rambova."

"Oh sure. Rambova. That's perfect. Just perfect. I know Ram."

Erik wasn't surprised. Clarette had told him that most all the people involved in the theater knew one another.

"I'll give Ram a call and see what he thinks. I can tell your wife that he called me and told me about the play."

Erik fought off the sensation of conniving, especially since this was to help Clarette fulfill her dreams. Surely there was no harm in giving his wife a little boost. "That's fine, Mr. Lepke."

"Hey, it's Lenny to you. I'm sure I'll be meeting you soon."

That done, Erik returned his attention to finishing the stories of the two raids he'd covered that day. He hated being away from Clarette so much and couldn't wait to get home.

———— ◉ ————

ERIK STEPPED INTO THE apartment late that evening to find an ecstatic Clarette.

"It's happened!" she said grabbing him and dancing about the kitchen. "It's finally happened. I was persistent and I never gave up, and it's finally happened!"

Her excitement filled the entire place, and made Erik's heart race. "Do you mind telling me what this is all about?" he said.

"This must be my miracle, Erik. Do you think God arranged this for me? Do you think it could be?"

"Without knowing the details, it'd be hard to say," he said, reaching down to give her glowing face a kiss. "How about if I hang up my hat and jacket and you tell me all about it?"

Over supper she told of receiving a phone call from an agent named Lenny Lepke who'd been contacted by Elmo Rambova. "Mr. Rambova is the one I told you about—with the funny horsey face and big wide grin. He's the only one who's said anything nice about my work."

Erik listened and nodded as he ate the baked fish and boiled potatoes which Clarette had cooked.

"I'm to take a copy of the script to Mr. Lepke tomorrow. Isn't that wonderful news? Mr. Lepke says he's ready to read anything. Now that's the kind of agent I want, Erik. He said nothing about me being unknown. Or a dame," she added in mocking tones. "I'm quite tired of being called a dame!"

With his stomach full, and the long, hectic day behind him, weariness suddenly encompassed Erik like a warm, heavy blanket. "That's about the most wonderful news I've ever heard," he said around a wide yawn.

"Oh, I'm sorry darling. You're beat and here I am going on and on."

"You have every right to be excited, Clarette. Don't apologize."

"But you've not told me a thing about your day."

"Nothing new. Izzy finally got his man at the olive oil warehouse, so I don't have to hang around that filthy rundown neighborhood again tomorrow."

"I'm glad of that." She stood up and took his hand. "You come into the living room and sit down and relax. I'll put something nice on the Victrola and the music will soothe you."

"But you need help..."

"Nonsense," she told him. "I'm so wound up, I could clean up the kitchen four or five times tonight."

Erik settled into the easy chair and attempted to read a new novel, but the music and the sounds of Clarette humming and working in the kitchen lulled him quickly to sleep. Later, he barely remembered her rousing him to go to bed. And as he slept, thoughts of how happy he'd made Clarette continued to dance through his brain.

ONCE ERIK WAS ASLEEP, Clarette read through her script one more time, smoothing out rough spots and checking for overlooked errors. The thrill of receiving the phone call from Lenny Lepke had almost erased the terrible experience of that afternoon at the Allmont Hotel. If the raid had been a few minutes sooner, Erik would have discovered his wife in that speakeasy. And it was common knowledge that clients as well as proprietors and employees, were all carted away together. No distinctions were made.

She was still shaken when she arrived later at Grandmother Vanderpool's, and her intuitive grandmother insisted there must be something wrong. Clarette could only answer that she'd been putting all her efforts into finding a home for her play. "The strain I'm under is a bit much," was her lame reply.

Grandmother Vanderpool had studied Clarette with intense concern. "Clarette," she'd said, "I hope you're not taking matters into your own hands. God wants you to be diligent with your work, but you can't *make* things happen."

"I wish someone would tell me how to know the difference," she snapped back. "God seems to change the rules every day."

Softly, Grandmother Vanderpool replied, "And how much time are you spending studying the Rule Book?"

Clarette purposely cut the visit short. It seemed to her that Christians spent all their time telling everyone else how to live.

But now—now she could tell her grandmother that she'd not taken matters into her own hands. This call from Lenny Lepke was her miracle from God. She was sure of it! And she'd not had a thing to do with it.

The next morning, Clarette was at the door of the Lepke Agency as soon as it opened. "Mr. Lepke is expecting you," said the polite secretary. *What a refreshing change*, Clarette thought as she entered the executive office. The trappings here were much more posh than the other offices she'd been in lately. This bouncy, nervous little man was obviously more well-heeled. Probably due to his optimistic attitude. While everyone else twiddled their thumbs and lamented, this man was out there going strong. Just what she needed.

After introductions, Lenny explained that he'd heard good things concerning *Journey's End* while talking with his friend, Mr. Rambova. Not only did he accept the copy that she had in hand, he also asked for a rundown of the plot, which she gave most gladly.

He nodded as she talked and then said, "Sounds good, Mrs. Torsten. Tell you what, I'll read this tonight and give you a call tomorrow. How's that?"

"Fine. Thank you." She stood to go. "I appreciate your taking the time."

He waved away her comment. "Think nothing of it. I may be thanking you before it's all over."

True to his word, Lenny called the next day with the news. "I've read the script, Mrs. Torsten. I like it. I want to handle your work, and I'm going over to see Ram this afternoon to give him the first shot at it. I think he'll snap it up like a doggie with a new bone."

Delirious with joy Clarette danced around the apartment hardly daring to believe it was really true. Laughing to herself she plopped down onto the davenport. "Mrs. Exa Belle Traeger," she said out loud, "I do believe I'll send you a set of gold embossed tickets to my opening night!"

Chapter 19

"We're opening at the Majestic in August, Grandmother."

"The Majestic?" Clarette could hear surprise in her grandmother's voice on the other end of the telephone line. "That's not too shabby for a first."

"Both my agent and the producer are wild about the play. And it doesn't make a bit of difference to them that no one knows my name."

"Have you told your father about all this good news?"

Clarette winced. Why did her grandmother always have to bring up difficult details? "I thought I'd wait until the casting is finished and things are really underway. You know, after all the preliminaries."

"You're going to be a busy young lady for the next few weeks. I don't know how you and Erik ever have time to see one another."

Clarette didn't want to admit how difficult it had been. She'd spent hours with Mr. Lepke and Mr. Rambova in the past couple of weeks going over every detail of the contract and the script. They assured her she'd have a say in the casting, which was extremely important. The contract was fair, and more than she'd ever hoped for. Erik, however, had been strangely quiet lately. She assumed he was just tired. "When this play makes us a mint," she told him one evening, "then you won't have to work so hard."

In answer to her grandmother's prying comment, she merely said, "We find special ways of being together. Sometimes we even meet at the automat and have lunch together." It wasn't a lie. They had done that once.

"I'm sorry I can't talk longer," she told her grandmother. "But you caught me just as I was leaving to go downtown."

"I understand, Clarette," came the kind reply. "I know this is a special time for you."

Just as Clarette hung up the phone and grabbed her hat, the phone rang again. To her surprise it was Gaven MacIntyre in Tulsa. While they'd received a couple letters from Gaven and Tessa, it was strange for him to place a long-distance call. On his schoolteacher salary, and with Tessa attending university, they didn't have extra money for such luxuries as long- distance calls. As usual, the static was horrendous.

"Say there, Clarette, do you two ever stay home? I've been trying to reach you for three days."

She laughed. "We haven't been home much in the past few weeks. There's a lot going on. Did you need to talk to Erik?"

"Yeah. Tell him I think I've found something."

The snap and sizzle of the static forced her to hold the receiver away from her ear. "Tell him you've found what?"

"There's a magazine starting up in Tulsa and they really need good editorial people, Clarette. This would be perfect for the two of you."

Poor Gaven. So that was it. He's been wanting Erik back in Tulsa ever since they left. "Thanks so much for the tip, Gaven, but my play's being produced here on Broadway and things are exploding for Erik and me just now."

"Oh. Sorry, I didn't know. Erik's note... I mean."

"Note? What note?"

"He must have written it before your good news came through."

"What did his note say, Gaven?" Clarette hadn't known of any note that Erik sent to Gaven. Why would he have written without telling her? Gaven seemed hesitant to explain.

"He just said to keep my eyes open for something popping out here, so that's what I did. He sounded a little fed up with the big city newspaper."

"That's understandable. He's been working terribly hard. But my play will change all that."

"That's great news about your play. Congratulations. Tessa and I are both very happy for you. Be sure to send us all the great reviews." He paused a moment waiting for the static to clear, then added. "No need to tell Erik I called."

That certainly went without saying. She thanked him again for calling and hung up.

As the subway whisked her downtown, she became even more determined that she would do everything in her power to help her play be a success. Erik needed a rest more than she'd ever imagined.

———◉———

THE CALL FROM LENNY at Erik's desk at the *American* came as a surprise. After all, Lenny was dealing with Mrs. Torsten, not Mr. Torsten. Erik had agreed to review the contract with Clarette, but other than that he knew little or nothing about what was going on. Since Erik spent so little time at his desk, he was surprised the man had even caught him there.

"Mr. Torsten," Lenny said, "how do you like the way things are going with your wife's play?"

Puzzled, Erik answered with a simple, "Fine. Everything's fine."

"We've got a good producer," Lenny continued. "Not one who's had a ton of hits, but he holds his own."

"Yes?" What was this man driving at?

"Tell me, Mr. Torsten, did I happen to mention there'd be a little fee for my services?"

"You didn't tell me, but I saw the contract which states your percentage."

"That's the formal agreement, Mr. Torsten, but since this is such a special case, I'm going to need a little more just to keep the deal moving. Know what I mean?"

"I have no idea what you mean." Erik's hands were turning clammy. He clenched and unclenched his fist. "Why don't you spell it out?"

"You got my address there?"

Erik still had the business card on his desk. "I have it. The Cordonelle Building on Fifty-Third."

"Meet me on the top floor in an hour."

"See here, Lepke, I have work to do."

"Did your little wife tell you they're getting ready to cast the play?"

"Of course she told me."

"You want the casting to continue, don't you?"

Anger smoldered deep inside Erik's gut. This little guy had better think twice if he thought he could pull any funny business. Taking a breath Erik forced himself to calm down. He could say no more over the phone; every word was overheard in the busy newsroom. He had no choice but to agree to meet with Lepke and get this little situation taken care of quickly.

"I'll be there."

"Now you're talking. See you in an hour."

Hanging up, Erik went back to the story in his typewriter, but he couldn't concentrate.

"What's up, Torsten. You look upset." It was Hank Maxwell standing in front of Erik's desk. "Everything going all right with your wife's play?"

Didn't this guy have any work to do? He was the last person Erik wanted to talk to. "Everything's fine, Maxwell. But thanks for asking."

Erik wondered if Hank Maxwell knew that this agent was a greedy fellow who was going to demand a little extra cash on the side. As soon as he thought it, he dismissed the idea. No sense borrowing trouble.

After getting rid of Hank, Erik made a quick exit. It wasn't difficult since Sid had pretty much given him free run of the place since the first day. He'd turned in so many scoops, Sid trusted him explicitly.

The Cordonelle Building was off lower Broadway. As he walked that direction in the summer heat, Erik found himself praying. Something he'd not done a lot of lately.

"Top floor," he muttered to himself as he entered the lobby. "What am I supposed to do when I get there?" The directory notated the Lepke Agency on the tenth floor, but the top floor was the fifteenth. When the door clattered open, he told the elevator operator, "Top floor."

"Yes sir," he said smartly. "Top floor it is." His tone made it sound like some kind of special place.

The elevator door opened onto a large opulent office area set with furnishings reminiscent of the Vanderpool estate. Soft oriental rugs, brass lampstands, Tiffany shades, and massive pieces of carved mahogany furniture gave the room a surreal effect. Who did this agent know?

"You're Mr. Erik Torsten?" asked an attractive young lady at the desk.

"I am."

She motioned toward a set of ornate double doors. "Go on in. They're expecting you."

They? Erik moved toward the door which opened on an equally well-furnished room. Leaning against the wall near the windows was a small man who must be, from Clarette's description, Lenny Lepke. But behind the desk sat the thick-necked, broad-shouldered Big Frenchy DeMange and there were those hate-filled eyes Erik knew he'd never forget.

"Ah, Mr. Torsten," came Big Frenchy's raspy voice. "We meet again. Only under different circumstances. At least now you won't be snapping any photographs with that camera of yours." He waved to a nearby chair. "Sit down. Make yourself comfy."

"What is this?" Erik demanded, not moving toward the chair.

"Now now. No need to get riled up." Big Frenchy made a tent of his pudgy fingers. "So, you're the bum who knows Izzy Eisenbaum's every step. Sort of his shadow so to speak. I understand Izzy and Moe both savor your type of coverage. Those boys lap up notoriety."

Erik had heard stories about the gangsters that the easy money from illegal liquor had spawned. But until now it had all been hearsay. Fine works of art hung on the walls, heavy rich draperies at the windows, gold pen and ink set on the desk. Big money here. Well, he had no money to add to their coffers, and told the man as much.

Big Frenchy gave a cold laugh. "Good enough. Because we don't want your money, Mr. Torsten. We want something that's easy for you to give. Don't cost nothing. All we want from you is a little information—at least for the time being anyway."

Erik felt himself tense up. "What kind of information?"

"Tips, Mr. Reporter Man. Tips like the little fat guy gives you. Tips to prevent me from being front page news again any time soon."

Giving a shrug, Erik said, "You can follow him just like I do. It's not difficult."

"Yeah, but I ain't got no time for such foolishness," Big Frenchy retorted. "My many businesses—which by the way includes a new Broadway play for which I have put up the cash—keep me much too busy to keep watch on a little flea like Izzy Eisenbaum."

Erik felt a wave of nausea pass over him. So Clarette's play was being financed by this kind of dirty money. If she knew, it would destroy her.

"Our part in the deal," the man continued, "is to produce a little play, and even throw in two or three good reviews as an added goodwill bonus." After another raspy laugh he added, "I got a few willing newsmen who'll do just that for a small fee."

Erik could hardly believe this man had that much power. Or that so many people could be bought off. He shook his head. "I'm sorry but I can't help you."

"Don't be too hasty now. Take your time and think about it."

"I can't help. I've asked to be taken off of Izzy's trail." That was only half a lie, because Erik had been planning to ask Sid that very thing. He just hadn't found the opportunity yet.

"Then ask to be put back on Izzy's trail. Simple." Big Frenchy spread his sausage-sized hands to show how simple. "Now our hard-working young agent here will call you tomorrow for your answer." Motioning to Lenny, he added, "Lenny? Kindly show the man out."

"My pleasure, sir."

Before the elevator delivered Erik back down to the lobby, he was already hatching a plan to get out of this mess. Some of the raids Izzy made were small and inconsequential. Izzy, who loved the thrill of the chase, had no preference of large or small busts. He hit them all. Maybe, just maybe, Erik could feed bits of information on the smaller ones and still keep Big Frenchy happy. It was worth a try.

The opening of *Journey's End* was so important to Clarette. What would it do to her if it were to suddenly close down?

Chapter 20

Clarette sat on the third row of the darkened theater. Electric fans did little to ease the sweltering heat. Beside her sat Elmo Rambova with a clipboard on his lap. Most of the lead parts had been filled, and now they were simply going through the group of stragglers looking for bit players.

"I still think John Barrymore would be the best choice for the male lead," Elmo said in a low voice.

Clarette could scarcely believe her ears. The only man in America more sought after than baby-faced young John Barrymore was the moving picture sensation Rudolf Valentino. "Can you get him?" she asked.

"Hmm?" Elmo riffled through a few sheets of paper.

"Can you get him? John Barrymore?"

"Naw. I think he's in London just now."

Being a bit bolder, she said, "Can he be called back?"

Elmo shook his head. "I think he's in some show over there."

"Oh," she said. But it didn't really matter. She was happy enough just having her play produced at the Majestic. Who needed John Barrymore? She continued to be amazed at how she'd had a say in all the casting. Elmo and Lenny both treated her like a queen. She'd never heard of such a thing. Most writers had little or no say in their productions.

Later that same afternoon, they listened as two different actors tried out for the lead and Elmo gave his opinion, but in the end asked which she preferred. In this instance she agreed with him, but nevertheless was flattered to be asked.

On her way to the subway kiosk that evening she happened to pass another theater where the billboard standing out front caught her eye. Stopping amidst the busy street she stared at it a moment. The upcoming play, *Clair de Lune*, starred the handsome young John Barrymore. She passed by here nearly every day, but she'd not paid much attention. Perhaps the show just opened.

How strange. Why would Elmo have made such a statement about not being able to get Barrymore? Trying to shrug it off, she reasoned that Elmo didn't get out much. Perhaps he did think John Barrymore was still in London. But anyway, what difference did it make?

———●———

BY THE END OF THAT week, rehearsals were fully underway. Each day she sat in the same third row holding a battered, marked-up copy of the script, watching carefully over every word and every nuance, and every stage entrance and exit. Hearing the words she'd written being spoken on this great stage filled her with awe.

Indeed, everything in her life would have been absolutely perfect except for Erik. She was having difficulty understanding his attitude recently. If she didn't know better she would have thought he was angry with her. But that was silly. Why would he be angry with her?

She'd not had time to read the newspapers lately, and he said little or nothing about what was going on at the *American*. When she asked him, he brushed off the subject. She chalked it up to weariness. But the other evening when she pressed him about Izzy and the ongoing raids, he snapped at her. Her darling Erik who'd never been upset with her a day in their whole first year of marriage—he snapped at her. She was at a loss to understand it. And they saw each other so little, there was no time to get to the bottom of it.

But after her play was a hit, then she planned to make him quit that hectic job. Obviously, running all over New York was wearing him to a frazzle.

NORMA JEAN LUTZ

She'd bumped into Herta in the hallway a few days earlier, and of course Herta said the polite thing about missing her and Erik at church. *Church.* Who in the world could think about church at a time like this? But she didn't say that. She simply thanked her for her concern. And then asked Herta to please tell Pastor and Mrs. Roswald hello for her. Surely once the play was up and running, her life would return to normal again.

***

ERIK WAS ALL TOO FAMILIAR with the brassy taste of fear which lies on a person's tongue and never goes away. He'd experienced it nearly every day during the war. But that was long ago. He never thought he'd ever taste it again. And hadn't. Not even when he was rescuing Clarette from the clutches of the Ku Klux Klan. Until now.

Every day he hated himself a little bit more for having been so dull-witted as to fall for such a silly hoax. He could hardly bear to listen to Clarette talk about the play. She still believed it was real, when in fact, from beginning to end, the whole thing was a sham. And all because he had jumped in and attempted to help. Who in New York, he wondered, wasn't working for Big Frenchy and his ilk.

He was pretty sure that Hank set him up by giving him the name of an agent who was a known patsy for Big Frenchy, and now his co-worker was having fun watching Erik squirm. The fact that Lenny Lepke never called except when Erik was in the office, indicated that Maxwell was feeding the guy information. Erik had fully underestimated the ruthlessness of Hank Maxwell.

For a time, Erik attempted to release only information regarding inconsequential raids. But Big Frenchy became more and more demanding. At one point Erik told him, "Foiling every raid is only going to make Izzy suspect me, and once he does, your inside track will disappear."

"You just get the information to me," he growled, his puffy face growing red, "and I'll decide which ones will be foiled."

More than once, Erik had started out toward the nearest precinct station to turn himself in as an informant, but then he thought of Clarette and lost his courage. Opening night was only a few days away. Once they got through opening night, then he'd decide where to go from there. After all she'd been through, she at least deserved a gala opening night

Meanwhile, he'd asked Sid to put him on other assignments. "Yeah, yeah, I hear you," Sid replied, waving his cigar. "I know you're sick to the teeth of the raids, but you mapped out this route, and I need you to stick with it for just a few more weeks."

———————⊙———————

DURING THE SECOND WEEK of intense rehearsals, Clarette happened to overhear a snippet of a conversation backstage that gave her an uneasy feeling. One actor was asking another if he'd ever worked for someone as lax and as inattentive to detail as Rambova. The other insisted he had not.

Clarette had nothing against which to measure Elmo's actions, but she couldn't help but wonder if other writers were required to act as quasi-directors. The grueling schedule was wearing her down to almost nothing. She barely had time to think.

Also, during the second rehearsal week, actors were beginning to nitpick at one another and Elmo did nothing to maintain peace or restore order. Finally at lunch one day, Clarette felt she had to get away. Grabbing a hot dog from the vendor outside the theater, she walked to Bryant Park and sat down under a shade tree to think and rest. But no sooner had she sat down when Shanks appeared out of nowhere.

"Miss Clarie, where you been? I done been looking for you all over the place for days."

"Hello, Shanks," she said with little enthusiasm. Bad timing. She desperately needed to be alone to sort things out. "I'm sorry you couldn't find me. I've been hiding inside a dark theater."

"Why?" The lanky boy dropped his shoeshine box to the ground and sat on the bench beside her.

"Why indeed." She was beginning to wonder the same thing herself. "My play is being produced, Shanks. A play that I wrote."

"Gollee. Right on Broadway?" He twisted his old fedora in his hands.

"Right on Broadway."

"Which one?"

"You mean which theater?"

He nodded.

"The Majestic. West Forty-Fourth."

Suddenly Shanks' animated face clouded and he shook his head. "Miss Clarie, you don't want to have no dealings with that place."

"What is it, Shanks? What do you know?" Here was someone she could trust with absolute confidence. Nothing passed by the ears of young Spindle-Shanks.

"Bad money what runs it."

"Bad money, huh? Whose?"

"Big Frenchy DeMange. He gots his fingers in that place and plenty other things. Mostly hootch."

"But my play?" she muttered almost to herself. "That doesn't make any sense."

"Big Frenchy's why I was looking for you."

"What are you taking about? All I know about DeMange is that he was busted in a big raid a while back."

"Big Frenchy don't like his picture took, I can tell you that much. Mr. Torsten's a nice man, so I was sure he didn't know much about the mobs."

Clarette felt her stomach tighten into a new knot. "Erik? What's Erik got to do with any of this?" Then she remembered the photo of Big Frenchy on the front page of the *American*, and Erik's remark about the man with the evil eyes. Somehow this mobster found a way to get to her husband for revenge.

"I seen your mister going into Big Frenchy's building where he gots his penthouse up on the top floor."

"What building is that, Shanks?" As if she didn't already know.

"The Cordonelle."

"Where the Lepke Agency is located?"

"That Lepke..."

"Don't tell me. He's one of Big Frenchy's patsies."

Shanks nodded. "They all in cahoots, Miss Clarie. I was sure your mister didn't know."

"No, Shanks. My mister had no earthly idea." What agony Erik must be suffering. No wonder he'd been so quiet. "I guess I should have named my play *Hagar*."

"What's that, Miss Clarie?"

"Nothing Shanks. Just something the Lord tried to tell me several months ago." Dovey had explained to her so clearly about how Abraham's faith got "tired," as Dovey put it, so he force the situation by turning to Hagar.

"Ishmael was not the child of Promise," Dovey had said. And obviously *Journey's End*, soon to open at the Majestic, was not her "child of promise" either—no matter how desperately she wanted it to be. How long had her conscience been nagging her? How long had she been ignoring the warning signs?

And Grandmother had been right all along. "Examine your motives," she'd said, but Clarette refused to listen. She wanted her play produced so desperately, and as a result Erik became the lamb led to the slaughter.

Lepke and Rambova had been bought off with easy money. Whether or not Lepke was an agent was debatable, but Rambova had probably never produced a play in his life. No wonder the man had no idea where John Barrymore was playing. She and Erik were tangled in a sticky web. *Now what should I do, Lord?*

"Shanks," she said as she fumbled in her purse for a pencil and pad, "you are a dear, dear friend. I'll never forget you for this." She scribbled a note on the paper. "I need one more favor from you."

"Anything for you, Miss Clarie."

"Go to the back-stage door of the Majestic and hand them this note. Tell them it's for Mr. Rambova. It just says I've gone home ill. This'll buy some time for Erik and me. Will you do that?"

He gave her a bright smile. "As good as done, Miss Clarie."

She didn't have much money on her, but she found a bill and tucked it into the pocket of his frayed shirt. "No," he protested, "I wants to do this for you."

She patted the pocket. "And Shanks I want to do that for you. I may not see you for a while." This boy was a gift from God if ever she'd seen one. "From a friend to a friend. Agreed?"

He nodded. "If you say so." Picking up his box he turned to her and said, "I sure is glad to know Mr. Torsten's innocent."

"I'm not sure how innocent he is now, but he was certainly unsuspecting."

———— ◦ ————

ERIK LOOKED UP FROM his desk as the door to the newsroom flew open. He was shocked to see his wife barreling toward him with her arms waving. Every eye in the newsroom was riveted in her direction.

"Erik, Erik! Elmo's scheduled our first dress rehearsal for this afternoon. I had no idea it was coming so soon. You've got to come and watch. I need you to be with me."

"Clarette, I can't..."

"Hey, Sid's my friend. I'll ask him if you can leave. It'll only take us about an hour."

"Wonder who rules the roost at the Torsten home?" came a wisecrack from behind Erik. "It sure ain't the rooster," croaked another. Snickers and muffled laughter sounded around the room.

Erik watched stunned as Clarette rushed into Sid's office, was inside only a moment, and came bounding back out. "See? Nothing to it." She grabbed his hat off the rack by his desk and set it on his head and took his hand. "In this city, Erik, you'll soon learn you can get somewhere only if you have the right connections. Come on now."

Bewildered, he stood up just as she whispered, "Hurry. I'll explain later."

Now he knew.

In the hall, she pointed him to the stairwell and he obediently followed. "We'll take a taxi to the apartment," she said as they tripped down the stairs, "The subway might be too dangerous. I figure no one will suspect we're gone at least until tomorrow, but no sense taking any chances."

Out on the street he hailed a taxi and they tumbled in breathlessly.

"How'd you find out?" he asked pulling her close to him.

"Shanks helped me put it some of it together, but I had a feeling all along something wasn't quite right."

"And pray tell, what did you say to Sid?"

She smiled. "I told him my husband was being blackmailed by a gangster and we were leaving town, but we'd give him the story later."

Erik laid his head back on the seat and laughed. That was the moment he realized that awful taste of fear was totally gone.

At the apartment, they threw clothes into suitcases while Erik explained about Hank giving him the name of Lenny Lepke and the ensuing blackmail setup.

"I'll leave a note for Herta explaining that we've left. She'll be more than happy to pack up the rest of the things to send to us."

Erik straightened up from where he was bent over his open bag. "And tell me, Mrs. Torsten. Exactly where is it that she'll be sending our things?"

"Why home, of course."

"Home? Bartlesville?"

She came up behind him and put her arms around him. "No silly. Home to Tulsa. Isn't that where you want to be? Isn't that why you sent Gaven that note? There's a new magazine starting up there, and I hear they're looking for writing talent—talent such as the Torsten team possesses."

Erik turned around to hold her close. "Clarette we've been keeping a lot from one another lately."

"But no more."

"No more." He agreed, kissing her softly. "Returning to Tulsa—is that what you want, too?"

She nodded. "I found you there, and I found the Lord there. I realize now I felt more at home in Tulsa than I have in any other place. That's where we belong."

Laughing, he said, "It's a cinch I'm not cut out for New York."

"Maybe I'm not either." Pulling away, she said, "Now Mr. Torsten in case you've forgotten, we're in a dreadful hurry."

Chapter 21

The clacking of the wheels and soft rocking of the train had lulled Clarette into a half sleep. Erik was dozing peacefully. Periodically she glanced over at his handsome face as he slept. Earlier at the St. Louis stopover they had placed calls to Herta and to Grandmother Vanderpool to let them know where they were. Grandmother insisted that she would go to their apartment and help Herta pack up their things.

When Clarette told her Grandmother, "You were right. You were right about everything," her grandmother simply replied, "I didn't want to be right, Clarette. All I ever wanted was for you and Erik to be safe in God's arms."

What a blessing she was.

"Clarette?" came Erik's voice from beside her.

So he wasn't asleep, but his eyes were still closed. "Yes?"

"What do you think they'll do about the play?"

"I have no idea. If they don't want to blow their cover, I guess they'll have to open." Then she added, "But the way they were handling it, it'll probably bomb."

He was quiet then. "Erik?" she said.

"Yes?"

"How did we get so far off track?"

"I've been asking myself the same thing." He opened his eyes now and sat up.

"Grandmother asked me if I was taking matters into my own hands. Perhaps I was. I really wanted that play to open. I guess I wanted it too much."

"You didn't have to take matters into your own hands, my dear. Your husband did that for you."

She tucked her arm into the crook of his. "I can hardly believe the lengths you went to in order to help me get what I thought I wanted. I'm amazed at the depth of your love." She laid her head contentedly on his shoulder. "From now on I'll be very careful of what I tell you I want. There's no telling what you might do." After a moment, she added, "Perhaps that was it. My selfish desires were what pulled us down."

"Hey now, don't forget you had a husband who was gloating over bylines and scoops. I thought I was pretty hot stuff there for a while until Hank Maxwell jerked the slack out. He knew the right bait for this mouse." He shook his head. "And I thought I couldn't be bought. What a joke that was."

"We were both wrong then." Clarette gave a little sigh. She was so sure the whole mess had been all her fault. Looking back, she realized that much of her intense drive was a result of wanting to show everyone back in Bartlesville. That realization filled her with shame—a shame that could be erased only by God's redeeming grace.

"When we get home to Tulsa," she suggested, "let's make a resolution."

"What kind of resolution?"

"Resolved," she said grandly, "that Clarette and Erik Torsten will never become too busy for the Lord, or for one another."

"My darling you have great wisdom." He planted a kiss on her nose. "Now come with me to the dining car. We have time before reaching Tulsa for me to buy dinner for the most beautiful and talented lady in the world."

"Erik Torsten, one compliment from you is worth a dozen hit plays on Broadway!"

Norma Jean Lutz Bio

Norma Jean Lutz's writing career began professionally in the 1970s when she enrolled in a writing correspondence course. Since then, she has had over 250 short stories and articles published in both secular and Christian publications. The full-time writer is also the author of over 50 published books under her own name and many ghostwritten books. Her books have been favorably reviewed in *Affair de Coeur, Coffee Time Romance, Romance Reader at Heart, and The Romance Studio* magazines, and her short fiction has garnered a number of first prizes in local writing contests.

Norma Jean is the founder of the Professionalism In Writing School, which was held annually in Tulsa for fourteen years. This writers' conference, which closed its doors in 1996, gave many writers their start in the publishing world.

A gifted teacher, Norma Jean has taught a variety of writing courses at local colleges and community schools, and is a frequent speaker at writers' seminars around the country. For eight years, she taught on staff for the Institute of Children's Literature. She has served as artist-in-residence at elementary schools, and for two years taught a staff development workshop for language arts teachers in schools in Northeastern Oklahoma.

As a writer who loves writing for teens, and hanging out with teens, Norma Jean has launched the **Clean Teen Reads** website and blog. Lots of fun stuff for teens! Check it out here:

www.CleanTeenReads.net[1]

The Site for Teens Who Love Books and Stories

---

1. http://www.CleanTeenReads.net

Other Titles by Norma Jean Lutz

The Tulsa Series

#1 *Tulsa Tempest* (Christian historical romance)
#2 *Tulsa Turning* (Christian historical romance)
#3 *Tulsa Trespass* (Christian historical romance)
#4 *Return to Tulsa* (Christian historical romance)

The Norma Jean Lutz Classic Collection

1. *Flower in the Hills* (a sweet teen romance)
2. *Tiger Beetle at Kendallwood* (a sweet teen romance)
3. *Rockin' into Romance* (a sweet teen romance)
4. *Oklahoma Exile* (a sweet teen romance)
5. *Forever is Over* (a pre-teen novel about friendship)
6. *Lingering Dreams* (a sweet teen romance)

Teen Coming-of-Age Action Adventure Novels

Brought To You By The Color Drab
A Noble Cause: An Honorable Man Upholds a Noble Cause

Don't miss out!

Visit the website below and you can sign up to receive emails whenever Norma Jean Lutz publishes a new book. There's no charge and no obligation.

https://books2read.com/r/B-A-ZJGT-NOHYC

BOOKS 2 READ

Connecting independent readers to independent writers.